THE ADVENT OF CHIP DOOLIN

BY
NEAL D. BOGOSIAN
ILLUSTRATIONS BY DAVID SAAD

Outskirts Press, Inc.
Denver, Colorado

This is a work of fiction. The events and characters described herein are imaginary and are not intended to refer to specific places or living persons. The opinions expressed in this manuscript are solely the opinions of the author and do not represent the opinions or thoughts of the publisher. The author has represented and warranted full ownership and/or legal right to publish all the materials in this book.

** Some of these stories originally appeared in the national publication Vintage and Classic Baseball Collector

The Adventures of Chip Doolin
All Rights Reserved.
Copyright © 2011 Neal D. Bogosian
Illustrations by David Saad
v3.0

This book may not be reproduced, transmitted, or stored in whole or in part by any means, including graphic, electronic, or mechanical without the express written consent of the publisher except in the case of brief quotations embodied in critical articles and reviews.

Outskirts Press, Inc.
http://www.outskirtspress.com

ISBN: 978-1-4327-7057-0

Outskirts Press and the "OP" logo are trademarks belonging to Outskirts Press, Inc.

PRINTED IN THE UNITED STATES OF AMERICA

Prologue

Get comfortable...and let me tell you about a man named *Doolin*. Chip Doolin was his name and he was one of the finest gentlemen to ever play the game of baseball, and boy could he hit! I know because I saw him. I was there, and let me tell you right now – before we go any further – all the stories are true! He could hit a ball so far that it would cross state lines before it fell back down to earth; some say he even re-defined "a country mile" with his gargantuan homers. Chip was a real marvel and I am proud to say, he was also my friend.

One of the perks of being a sports journalist is that you get to go to every game. I had the fortune of seeing every inning Chip Doolin ever played. A real man, that farm boy was, and one of the strongest too! Pure, raw strength locked up in those bones and body of his. I remember when he first came up like it was yesterday, and I wish it *was* yesterday because I would love to re-live those days again, that is why you should all appreciate the time you have now, because you'll miss it when it's gone.

So pull up a chair and I'll tell you about the man who came before Babe Ruth, Hank Aaron and Mickey Mantle. A man who was too good to be put in any record book for mortals because all the records were his...and he had the aura of a God because he played like one. Sure, he had his flaws, but what man does not?

The Road to Detroit

WHACK! He swung the broken broomstick and the crab apple soared into the oblivious blue sky. He grabbed another from the pile and with the stick on his shoulder he gazed out into the open landscape. The sprawling farmland was his baseball diamond and the vast expanse of land was his outfield. The stump that rose from the earth about sixty feet, six inches away, that sometimes reminded him of the oversized bosom of his overweight aunt, was instead the pitcher's mound. That was where he saw Chief Bender staring in for the sign. He heard the roar of the crowd, the cheers and the jeers, and the smell of tobacco filled his nose. He saw "The Chief" wind and wield – a fast one coming and WHACK! Chip Doolin hit another crab apple into the deep blue sky, beyond the pumpkin patch, the spinach patch and the apple trees too.

"Dang it! We got some hay to get in! Let's get goin'!"

"Alright, Daddy, just a few more..."

"When you gonna give that silly game up, anyway? You ain't no ballplayer – you's a farmer! Your great granddaddy was a farmer. Your granddaddy was a farmer and your Daddy's a farmer – "

"But I don't wanna be no farmer, Daddy. Why do I have to be what you is? I desire a different sorta life. I wanna be a ballplayer," said Chip.

"Well, forgit it! Quit your dreamin'. That's all you is...you's a dreamer and this world ain't no dream. This can be a cruel place for them dreamers like you. It don't forgive you none for doin' it. You'll be eatin' chewed up corn cobs n' piggy ears if you don't stop, with a hole as big as your Aunt Clara's mouth in both your pockets. Now let's go, we got to ready the place for the gatherin' next week."

Chip hesitated. It just didn't seem right to go on doing what he knew he wasn't meant to do.

Never before had he challenged his father. He was always the good son and respected him; listened to his rules, advice and stories, and obeyed his orders like a good son should, but this time was different – this day. He awoke feeling older. Thrill, adventure and desire seized him in a way it never had.

Standing there in the middle of the family farm, his broomstick bat in one splintered hand and the hay fork at his feet, he was suddenly emboldened by a decision all his own. For the first time, Chip Doolin felt brave enough to take a step forward, defend his dreams and shed his adolescence.

"I ain't gonna be here next week, Daddy. I'm goin' away."

His father was already ten paces from him; ten paces en route to the barn, but he heard every word.

"What'd you say?" snapped his father, frozen in his tracks. He turned and glared at his only son. "What you mean you ain't gonna be here? Where's you gonna be?"

"I'm tryin' out for the Detroit ball club next week."

"Detroit? Ball club! You gone crazy! I'm gonna tell your Mama. She ain't gonna let you go – go n' grow up like them rogue people. Them ballplayers are all circus performers, n' crazy – like you actin' right now. I heard 'bout that Ruben Waddell fella! They say he's a nut! He chases fire engines in the middle o' ballgames! No way. My boy ain't no nut. You ain't goin'!"

"Yeah, I am!"

"No you ain't and that's that! I love ya too dang much to see my boy wear funny clothes n' – "

"Daddy, I ain't no kid no more – "

"Well, maybe so, but you're still my boy and I can still whoop you a good one...or – or at least try," said his father, after looking over the hulking size of his son.

"Hey! I'll make you a bet," said Chip, "that I can hit a crab apple all the way into Mr. Ferris' farm yard."

His father peered out across the farm and considered the proposition. "You can't do that! Ain't no one can do that! You gots a better chance o' seein' the cow climb a tree."

"Well, I can and if I do then I go to Detroit next week!"

Daddy Doolin was on the spot. He thought about the crazed wager, but only for a few seconds. "Fine! Like I say, you gone crazy at a tender young age. No way you hit a crab apple that far n' if ya do, I reckon I'll pay the dang train ticket."

"You mean it?"

"Yup. Cuz I know you ain't gonna hit it that long," said his father, resolutely folding his arms across his chest and waiting. "You got a better chance o' seein' our two cows reproduce n' give us a calf – but they're too dang old to do it no more."

Chip bent down and found one of the hardest crab apples he ever put his hands on.

"Now let's get this foolery over with so you can get back to pickin' that hay," said his father, who continued to talk and mutter odd nothings under his breath.

I think at that moment Chip knew he would never again work on a farm, and I'd like to think that he knew about the starry future that awaited him.

Chip gripped the shiny apple with pride. He gripped it with dreams flowing through his blood, with a special regard for the game of baseball, a boy's game played by men. He felt the adrenaline rush through his six-foot, four-inch frame like the locomotive that he hoped would bring him to Detroit.

He eyed the distant field. He saw Mr. Ferris laboring hard in his garden, the marauding farm dogs wandering in the prairie, and the boundaries he had to exceed more than four hundred feet away…and he saw Mr. Young. Cy Young was on the mound, staring him down. The Red Sox were ahead of the Tigers 7-3. The bases were full and it was the bottom of the ninth. Two men were already out and Chip Doolin was down to his last strike. He heard the noise and smelled the familiar smells of the ballpark all over again that wafted up through his nose; steamy hot dogs, roasted peanuts, leather and fresh cut grass. Ty Cobb was chanting him on from the third base line, "C'mon kid! You can do it! Look for the curve!"

Young checked the sign, and beneath the lid of his Red Sox cap, his beady, dark eyes zeroed in on Chip. In one determined motion, Young rocked back, kicked and threw. Chip's eyes widened. It was a fat one! He swung the stick with all the speed he could muster and WHACK! But this didn't deserve just one WHACK, but two! The crab apple soared and kept soaring, higher and higher and deeper and deeper, eclipsing and soaring over his Daddy's field and just when the apple became a dark dot in the sky, it came down and landed at the feet of Eleanor Ferris, the blue-eyed daughter of Mr. Ferris, whom Chip had fancied ever since he knew about the bond between a man and a woman; she was the heroine of his every fantasy, and the fact that the apple landed at *her* feet, signaled a very special coincidence to Chip, as if it was *supposed* to happen that way.

"I'm going to Detroit!" exclaimed Chip.

THE ADVENTURES OF CHIP DOOLIN

His father stood frozen and speechless. He was in utter shock, his jaw suspended somewhere between his Virginia farm and *Bennett Ballpark* in Detroit. There was a distant glimmer in Pop Doolin's eyes, for they had just registered an unfathomable feat. It was only then that he recognized his son's potential, as he mumbled in a hushed tone, "That there apple's got wings! That was a dang crab apple...my boy hit a crab apple farther than yonder..."

The next week arrived quickly and Chip found himself packing a small satchel for the long ride to Detroit. He packed his well-worn ball glove, along with a mental registering of some advice that his old friend Joe Miller had given him. Joe played for Toledo and Louisville in the American Association, in the mid 1880s. Chip never forgot the day that Joe gave him the glove and even now, it sent Chip to cherishing all of the knowledge of the game that must be tucked away in the web of the well-used mitt.

He packed the only clothes he owned – some odd garments that were either too small, had a hole or two, or were completely out of fashion. He also packed the photo of his hero – Cy Young, along with a rabbit's foot and the money from his savings, before sealing the satchel shut.

His parents were waiting in the kitchen to drive him to the station and see him off. It was his first trip away from home – away from his hometown of Somewhere, Virginia – and just before he was about to leave his bedroom, he overheard some light chatter outside his window.

"You believe Chip's goin' to Detroit? To try that silly game?"

"Never would have thought his Mama would let him go, as dumb as he is and all."

"Yeah, but those ballplayers are dumb too!"

"Yeah, and have ya heard about that Rube Waddell fellow?"

"Oh! The crazy one! He chases fire engines – leaves the mound in the middle of a game!"

"Yeah! Yeah! Chip ought to fit in fine – "

"But Chip couldn't hit a barn with a ball. How's he gonna throw it to first base?"

"How's he gonna hit? They gonna whiz that ball by him so fast, he'll get all dizzy and fall over like he was a tipped cow."

Laughter erupted and Chip hung his head in a sudden jolt of sadness, dejected and pained over the way his two friends perceived him, but he knew they were not friends any longer and he knew something else – he had to earn a spot on the Detroit club to prove them wrong and to prove he was not dumb;

to prove he had talent and the game of baseball was a game of strategy and wit.

It may have been just the medicine he needed, for vengeance seems to have a way of empowering a man, it gives him a reason to compete at the highest level. Just before tears welled up in his eyes, he heard his father calling, "Hey, Chipper! C'mon, you gonna miss the train!"

Chip Doolin, with the visor of his cap pulled down over his eyes, was on his way to Detroit, already carrying with him a courageous spirit and the determination of the victor.

⚾ ⚾ ⚾

When he stepped out onto the platform at the Detroit train station, he knew from the change in the air alone, that he was very far from the calm confines of his Virginia farm. There was a vibrant energy in the air, like the exhilaration one feels in a bustling city, one that made Chip want to conquer the world and not waste a single moment in the process.

Chip walked out of the station and boarded a horse and carriage that brought him to the ballpark. It was an unusually temperate day for late February, and the Tiger team decided to stay in Detroit for one more week before going down to Florida for spring training.

The park was pristine and magical from Chip's view, just as he had always dreamt; a kingdom of awe and fantasy where heroes were made, a perfect house for baseball.

He bravely walked through the gates, past the ticket booth and through the wide opening that led to the field.

Even the seats in the stands had an imperial luster that revealed the storied episodes and epic feats – all part of baseball lore – that had unfolded on the diamond below. Echoes and whispers of long batted balls and roaring crowds, like baseball spirits, seemed to be nestled everywhere, and when Chip arrived, they rose up to meet him.

After surveying his surroundings, he descended the stadium steps to field level.

"Hey, kid! How you gonna run the bases in those? Did ya make a trade for the hoofs of the horse you rode in on?" said a man standing next to the dugout.

Chip looked down at his worn and tattered leather work boots, the only shoes he owned. A boyish innocence shaded his cheeks when he looked back up to the man speaking to him. He was face-to-face with *Detroit Tigers* Manager, Hughie Jennings.

"Mac..." continued Jennings to his equipment manager, "get'em some spikes."

"Kay, boss."

"Your name Doolin?"

"Y – yes, sir...I – I am him."

"Well, I wanna see whatcha got, so Mac'll get ya ready. Joe Miller spoke pretty highly of you." He paused briefly then said, "You certainly got the size for this game, and we may need another first bagger for insurance. You ever play there before?"

"I – I'm mighty sure I can do it, Mr. Jennings," said Chip.

"Well, I hope you don't have as many holes in your bat and glove as you do in them boots and under your arm pits, or you'll be back wherever you came from by midnight tonight. Awlright, Mac. Take'em away."

"C'mon kid, let's get those flops o' yours fitted – "

"And give'em a better hat too! Make'em look like a ballplayer before he walks onto this field!" said Jennings.

"Kay, boss."

Soon after, Chip Doolin emerged from the dugout. He still wore his oil-stained trousers and his regular, three-button work shirt, but he now sported a new *Detroit Tiger* ball cap and a pair of shiny, black spikes.

"Well rookie, you're an inch closer to lookin' like a ballplayer!" said Jennings. "Now you look like a guy who came out of a garage and put on some spikes, instead of a guy who *lives* in one."

Chip looked out onto the ball field. They were all there: Ty Cobb, "Wahoo" Sam Crawford, George Moriarty, Donie Bush, Germany Schaefer, Matty McIntyre, "Wabash" George Mullin, Ed Willett and Ed Summers – the surprising young pitcher who, as a rookie, won twenty-four games the year before. They were practicing drills and exercising under the friendly sunshine and the same blue sky through which Chip had sent many a crab apple soaring. Only now he had to prove he could hit a *baseball*. You see, down on the farm – Chip's farm – real baseballs were a rare luxury!

The starry-eyed, seventeen-year old kid, from Somewhere, Virginia – somewhere no one here had heard of – was about to get his chance. He could count the number of times he held a real bat in his hands and threw a real ball, but he remembered everything that Joe Miller had taught him – the advice and the lessons, crafted into late night stories and early day ritual, days he would tell his father he was going fishing, but instead spent the afternoon learning about and being tutored on the mechanics of baseball.

When Chip stepped forward his legs shook like thunder. His first step on the field put him on the grass along the first base line, and with his next step, Chip Doolin landed into the annals of fate.

Wow, he thought, *I'm here. I'm here with the*

1909 Detroit Tigers.

However, while these big leaguers were letting Chip soak it all in from the foul line; while they grinned and smiled and gestured warmly toward the boy who was barely a man, aware of the wonder and awe that he was experiencing, it suddenly occurred to Chip that he had to shed the dazed and star-struck joy from his head and take command of himself, to come within his own and create his destiny here and now. He wisely knew that this was his one chance to make his dreamy fate a reality, a chance that may never come again. His aim was nothing less than the highest achievement he had ever imagined – next to his fascination with Eleanor.

I've gotta do this! I've gotta 'snap to' and prove them wrong!

He thought of Eleanor, and he thought of his two former allies, Jimmy and Clyde. The fire from these thoughts alone stirred him enough to walk over to the bat rack and grab one that he liked. He sampled a few before settling on one that felt best in his hands, one that most closely resembled the feel of a broken broomstick.

"Hey, kid!" said Ty Cobb, "that's *my* bat!" He laughed when he saw Chip freeze in embarrassment. Then Mr. Cobb offered, "It's okay, kid. You can use it. Just don't let me see you swing n' miss with it, or you'll bring me bad luck."

"Th – Thanks, Mr. Cobb! I – I promise I won't swing n' miss! I sure won't be no swing n' miss type. I got me a few things to prove to some folks back home. And I – I hope you'll be mighty proud after I'm done."

"Okay, kid!" said a laughing Cobb.

"Alright, boy! Let's see what you got!" yelled, Jennings. "Step in there and take some swings!"

Chip felt the adrenaline rush through his veins again. He remembered it was only last week that he sent a crab apple flying across the field before his Daddy's eyes, but when he remembered Eleanor, a different kind of excitement gripped him.

Gee, imagine what Eleanor might think if I made the Detroit Tigers! She's such a mighty sweet gal to be stuck on. But I'm gonna show Jimmy n' Clyde! I'm gonna show'em right now!

He stepped into the batter's box. Oscar Stanage was the catcher behind the plate and Ed "Twilight" Killian was on the mound. The players assembled in the field, dispersing themselves in a fashion ready to shag some balls. Chip dug into the batter's box just the way Joe Miller had taught him. He squeezed the handle of the bat, brought it back and focused all the concentration he had on the leather baseball in the pitcher's hand.

Killian looked in, wound and delivered.

This one's for you, Jimmy.

THE ADVENTURES OF CHIP DOOLIN

WHACK! Chip hit a towering drive that cleared the entire ballpark in left field!

Hughie Jennings scratched his head in amazement. "Geez!" he mumbled, "Glad we gave this kid some spikes, eh, Mac?"

"Yeah, boss."

Killian looked in again. The players in the field slapped their gloves with enthusiasm, looking forward to a workout at the expense of the newcomer. They all figured the first one must have been a fluke. Then there was another wind and another delivery.

This one's for you, Clyde.

WHACK! Chip hit another booming drive, this time clearing the center field wall by thirty feet! The players began motioning to one another, impressed by the display, and what a display it was! I remember after he hit that second one I was fumbling for my pen to write down his name. I immediately knew that his was a name I had better remember.

Killian got another sign from Stanage. He kicked and threw – a curve ball.

Joe said to wait on curves.

WHACK! Doolin whacked another over the left field fence, one that kept soaring out of sight.

That one was for you, Joe.

Chip went on to hit one for his Daddy and one for his Mama and another for all the ballplayers who were called 'dumb' and another for this cause and still one more for that cause, but he saved one more for someone special.

"Alright, Doolin. I see you can hit – I mean, *you can hit*! And you can hit'em far, by golly!" exclaimed Jennings. "Go grab your glove and take some at first."

"Uh, Mr. Jennings? Can I hit just one more?"

"One more? I don't think Ed has anything left to throw you! All's he's got is his arm to throw now. You think you can hit his arm over that there fence, Doolin?"

"Mr. Killian," pleaded Chip, "can you just throw me one more? I – I'd be most grateful, sir."

"Okay, kid. I'll throw one more just so you can embarrass me one last time for good luck."

"Th – thank you kindly, Mr. Killian! Thank you!"

"Hey, kid!" yelled Jennings, "Why one more?"

Chip shrunk a bit and removed his hat. Beneath bashful eyes he replied, "It's for someone real special, Mr. Jennings," and he nodded his head lightly, repeating, "someone real special."

"Oh, yeah? What's her name, Doolin?"

"Uh, Eleanor, sir. And she's a mighty fine one to be stuck on and I'd just be – "

"Alright, Ed...give'em one more for Eleanor. We might have to give *her* a contract to sign if she's the charm that's makin' you hit'em like they was canon bombs."

Chip gripped the bat, dug in and waited. The pitch came and the ball went. It was his longest drive of the day, sailing deep into the abysmal sky. After the mighty swing, Chip was smiling from cheek to cheek, as if his eyes had just seen Heaven.

That one there was for you, sweetheart!

"You must really like this dame, Doolin!" yelled Jennings.

The players, who were expecting a workout, instead were treated to an air show. The Major League home run leader in 1908 was National Leaguer Tim Jordan of Brooklyn, who hit twelve. The American League home run champ in 1908 was none other than the Tigers' own Sam Crawford, who hit seven round-trippers. Chip Doolin had just finished hitting more out of the ballpark than both of those totals combined!

As he walked down the first base line to take some grounders, some of the Tiger players came over to greet him and shake his hand, including Ty Cobb.

"You certainly didn't miss, kid, just like you said. Here...I want you to have this bat. It's yours. You deserve to keep it."

"Wow! Thanks, Mr. Cobb!"

"You bet, kid. What's your first name?"

"Chip. My name's Chip."

"Well Chip, keep hittin'em like that and we'll be

goin' to the World Series again."

Chip was filled with more elation than words could say, but later that evening, he tried to put it all in words when he sent a telegram to his parents that read:

> Deer Mom an Pop. Maid Detroit club. Sined player Contrak. Makin Money as First Bagger. Tel Joe. Have to work on grounders one hit me in noze. Be shure to tel Jimy an Clyde. Tel Eleanor I sed hi an I aint forgit her. Send Cloze wit no holes. Luv Chip.

Chip Doolin was now a member of the Detroit Tigers.

Opening Day

His heart raced at the sight of the people filling the stands; ardent baseball fans being shown to their seats by the attendants, wearing their best pressed clothes and donning straw hats, knit caps and bow ties – this was Opening Day. It was an afternoon away from the chores of life; the first excuse to bring spring clothes out from their winter hibernation and feel the rejuvenation of a new season. Chip Doolin had never played in front of a crowd. He had never done anything before an audience, except for opening birthday gifts in front of his Mom and Pop.

The baseball world had already bestowed something special upon the young Doolin throughout his first spring training – maturity. By now Chip had learned that friendship represented much more than ridicule: sincerity, honesty and loyalty were the true trademarks. His friends were suddenly the likes of Ty Cobb, Sam Crawford and the rest of the Tiger team.

Chip Doolin, the kid from Somewhere, Virginia, made quite a first impression on Tiger management, and his hitting antics in the spring training curcuit made a splash on sports pages across the nation. So it came as no surprise that Chip Doolin was named the Detroit Tigers Opening Day first baseman.

He still had the eyes of a child and the cheeks of a baby, and both were aglow when he jogged to the first base bag for pre-game grounders.

Doolin scraped the dirt with his spikes and tapped the bag twice, because Donie Bush told him it brought good luck, "You know. . . .like that expression 'knock on wood'?"

"I ain't never heard that before, Donie."

"Oh…well now you have. You tap that bag and it gets all the evil spirits out – "

"Oh! I sure don't want no evil 'round me. Thanks, Donie!"

Chip looked in front of the Washington Nationals dugout, where his eyes fell on the swift, sweeping motion and the wicked speedball of Walter Johnson, the opposing pitcher. He stared in awe of the fellow nicknamed, "The Big Train".

Doolin got so caught up in watching Johnson, he never saw the first ground ball come his way, and it bounced right through his legs.

"Hey Doolin!" yelled Tiger manager, Hughie Jennings.

"Yeah?" answered a despondent Chip.

"You see a stray ball anywhere? Maybe one that just went through your wickets! What the heck are ya doin'? Get them grounders!"

"Oh! Okay, sir! I – I'm mighty sorry! I missed that one."

"Oh, did you? I could o' swore you fielded it clean and touched the bag – pay attention to what's in front o' you. You'll get your chance at'em! And breathe, Doolin – breathe! That's one o' them automatic functions we was given. Don't let your nerves get in the way o' that cuz you just seen the man that throws the fastest ball on earth!" said Jennings.

Getting his chance to bat against Walter Johnson, however, was the last thing Chip Doolin wanted to do in his first big league game, but before he could find some extra courage, the plate umpire yelled, "Play ball!" and the crowd responded with thunderous applause.

⚾ ⚾ ⚾

When a majestic white cloud coasted over the bustling Washington ballpark, it cast a matching shadow on the ground, where the Washington club produced the game's first run in the bottom of the second. Clyde "Deerfoot" Milan tripled to left-center and came home on a single by Gabby Street, and

the capital city fans cheered with joy.

Washington had suffered through a dismal season and a seventh place finish the year before, and the hometown folks hoped for something better this year. Johnson had thus far set down the first six men he faced. When the top of the third inning came, Chip Doolin, batting seventh in the order, was set to lead off and make his first major league plate appearance.

Doolin's body shuddered as he walked slowly to the batter's box. He could feel the heat of thousands of eyes bearing down on him. His head was lowered, watching the movement of his own feet, as they made their way to home plate. He seemed unsure whether to be tentative or bashful, and I couldn't blame him, because Walter Johnson's fastball came in like a train and if someone had said he threw bullets, I'd have believed them!

On that first at-bat Chip was just trying to figure out how he should swing against Johnson. Should he swing for the fences? Protect the plate? Pray to the skies that he just get a piece of one? Dozens of converging emotions stacked one atop the other and they all registered on his face. I think he was the most nervous man on earth, but this was show time!

When he stepped into the batter's box, Chip was stepping onto center stage. As he dug in, his Tiger teammates cheered him on from the bench. His knees had a bad case of the shivers, and for a good reason. The man on the mound, about to throw that first pitch, was one of the best pitchers ever. In my book, he *was the best*!

The name, "Walter Johnson", was already finding its way around the league. After joining the Nationals in 1907, Johnson quickly established himself as a fireball pitcher with a quiet, humble, almost thoughtful demeanor. He was always friendly. He was always fast. In 1909, he was also a bit wild.

The fans were already expecting something big from Chip when he brought his hands back, steadied his bat and waited for Johnson's offering. The first pitch to Doolin nearly took off his head. It was a high fast one that Chip never even saw coming and if it were not for the catcher Gabby Street, the rookie's big league career may have ended then and there, with his name entered into the Baseball Almanac *without* an official at-bat and a 'hit-by-pitch' by his name; but fate had other plans. Before that ball even reached Doolin, the catcher yelled, "Watch it!" Only because of instinct did Chip stumble back out of the way and fall to the ground.

"Are you okay? Gee, I'm awfully sorry," came a voice.

The young Doolin looked up to see a worried and concerned Walter Johnson standing over him.

He had sprinted off the mound toward home plate as soon as he released the errant pitch.

"I – I think I'm okay," said Chip.

"C'mon Doolin! Get back in there and take some licks!" said Sam Crawford from the Tiger bench.

"Yeah, C'mon Chip! Shake it off! Johnson only threw that one to clean the wax outta your ears," said Ty Cobb.

Doolin got to his feet and wiped the dirt from his pants. He could still feel his knees shaking.

"Knock it outta the park, Doolin!" said a lonesome Detroit fan amidst the brewing Washington fanfare, but Chip's knees trembled so badly, he was worried he might not be able to run out of the batter's box.

Johnson returned to the mound and stared in for the sign. Doolin tapped his spikes with the bat, dug in and waited.

"Strike one!" yelled the umpire, on a ball that came so fast Doolin did not have the time to even flinch.

Then, "Strike two!"

When the next pitch came, Doolin swung with all his might, but the ball was already in the catcher's mitt. "Steerike three! Yer out!" He was Johnson's fourth strikeout victim.

The sullen Doolin walked the long path back to the dugout. It was not what Chip had planned in his first Major League at-bat.

"Get'em next time, kid," encouraged Cobb. "He's a tough one. One o' the best in the game."

Johnson went on to retire the next two Tiger men in order and the burly Washington hurler had a no-hitter through three innings.

⚾ ⚾ ⚾

The top of the fourth was interrupted by the boisterous arrival of United States President William Howard Taft, who waved to the clapping capacity crowd, before settling behind the home team dugout with a five-cent bag of roasted peanuts in his lap. The hefty President, with his thick, sloping moustache, double-breasted suit and top hat, nearly took up two seats.

Chip Doolin's first chance in the field did not come until the fifth inning. With the score still 1-0, Nationals' shortstop George McBride hit a ground ball that Chip almost turned into a circus stunt. It was a bumbling, bouncing grounder that he fielded, dropped, picked up, bobbled, and finally held on long enough to step on the bag, just in time to get the fleet-footed McBride.

"Hey Doolin, is that a hot potato you're handlin' out there?" yelled Jennings from the top step of the dugout.

"No, sir."

"Well, Doolin you're takin' that ball like it's got teeth. Did it go n' bite you somewheres?"

"No, sir. I just got a lil' mixed up – "

"Well, you're better than that, Doolin. That's why you're out there. Don't be as simple as a tree. I got too many bush leaguers who are all sorts o' trees. Can't have this forest get too dense, Doolin. Now relax n' go get'em!" said Jennings.

"Yessir," said Chip.

Washington pushed across another run in the top of the sixth, to make it 2-0. Gabby Street roped his second single of the game to left field, took second on Jack Lelivelt's sacrifice bunt and scored when Tiger starter George Mullin yielded a run-scoring double to Jim Delahanty.

Doolin came to bat again in the bottom half of the inning, while Johnson, to the delight of the Washington faithful, was still working on a no-hitter.

The Tiger rookie stepped up to the plate a bit more determined than before. He gripped the bat and cocked it back.

"C'mon kid!" came from the Tiger dugout, "Get us goin' here."

Johnson wound and delivered. It was another fastball and Doolin swung... *'SMACK!'* It was the sound of the ball hitting the catcher's mitt. Strike one. Johnson stared in for the sign, winded, wielded and delivered. Again, Chip swung.

'*SMACK!*' Strike two went blazing into the catcher's mitt; the ball was so fast it hissed past Doolin.

"Darn it!" said Chip aloud. His frustration and anger replaced any nervousness that remained. He stepped out of the batter's box. Determination was building in the sweat on his brow. He stepped back in the box with a start. He gripped the bat a little lighter and concentrated a little more. The pitch came. Doolin swung.

'*WHACK!*' He got hold of one and the left-handed Doolin hit a towering drive down the left field line. It soared high and long and it brought the crowd to their feet…but it bent foul into the stands.

"Do it again, Chip! You can do it!" yelled Donie Bush, the Tiger shortstop. "Choke up a bit!"

Chip choked up on the bat and stepped back in for another try. The crowd was buzzing after the long foul, so far the longest drive of the day. Johnson checked the sign, before kicking and dealing.

"Ball one!" yelled the ump. The pitch was outside and Chip nearly broke his swing to go after it, but the strength of his forearms resisted.

Both sides readied once more. The imposing Johnson toed the top of the pitching plate before he wound and threw. It was a curve ball, and Doolin waited as long as he could, but to no avail.

He swung and missed becoming Johnson's eighth strikeout victim and the inning was over.

The game remained 2-0 until the top of the ninth. Johnson took the mound with his no-hit bid still alive. He had retired twenty-four Tigers, striking out ten and walking five, with just three more outs to go for an Opening Day no-hitter. The crowd rose to its feet in anticipation, the excitement building, hoping for the final crescendo and a great start to the new season. They gripped their programs – programs autographed by Crawford, Johnson and others – they gripped them with fervor and hope, but their hopes were dampened when the first pitch of the inning from Johnson was belted by Ty Cobb into the right-center field gap. By the time the ball was retrieved and thrown back to the infield, Tyrus Cobb, "The Georgia Peach," was standing on third, Johnson's no-hitter was over and his shutout was now in jeopardy.

The next batter was Sam Crawford. Cobb danced off third. As soon as Johnson raised his leg to throw, Cobb was off and running for the steal of home.

The pitch came. Crawford swung and missed deliberately. The catcher, Street, dove for the plate with the ball in his hand. Cobb slid, and the two men collided. Dust swirled and clouded over the plate. When it settled, Gabby Street was on his back and the ball was on the ground. Ty Cobb was ruled safe and it was now a 2-1 ballgame.

Some harsh words were exchanged between Street and Cobb, one accusing the other of a spiking.

"...then you shouldn't block the plate!" yelled Cobb.

"You came in with your spikes up!" said Street.

"Then you're lucky they missed you."

On the next pitch, Crawford laid down a perfect drag bunt that rolled to a stop on the fair side of the first base line. He was now aboard at first.

Johnson fanned the next hitter, Matty McIntyre, on three pitches, for the first out of the inning – Johnson's eleventh strikeout of the game.

On the second pitch to the next batter, Germany Schaefer, Crawford stole second base ahead of Gabby Street's throw, who Hughie Jennings detected was still a bit wobbly from his collision with Cobb.

The next delivery from Johnson resulted in a ground ball to the right side. It was headed for the outfield, but Washington second baseman Jim Delahanty made a diving stop on the edge of the outfield grass. He lifted his body and threw, but the throw bounced in the dirt and Schaefer was safe at first – Crawford advanced to third on the play.

The Nationals were still two outs away from victory, and the next batter was the rookie, Chip Doolin.

His heart raced again. A base hit would tie the game. Washington skipper Joe Cantillon motioned to his outfielders from the top step of the dugout, positioning them straight away for Doolin.

Chip dug in, planting his back foot. He choked up on the bat, brought his hands back and waited for Johnson's pitch.

"Strike one!" yelled the umpire, on a fastball that nipped the outside corner.

Chip liked the looks of the next offering from Johnson and swung with all his might. "Strike two!"

Doolin stepped out of the box. He rested the bat on his shoulder and looked helplessly toward the ground. Then, suddenly, he had the odd inclination to pause and scan the faces of all the fans in the front rows. His eyes fell on one fan in particular.

"Oh my gosh!" said Chip aloud, "Eleanor!"

There was Eleanor Ferris, the farm girl from Somewhere, Virginia, but on this day she looked nothing like a farm girl. She was dressed like a lady of society, beautiful and glowing in the warm sunlight. The sight of her made Chip's heart feel the awkwardness of love, right in the middle of his first big league ball game.

"Hey, c'mon! Play ball!" said the umpire, but Doolin remained, basking in his own surprise, his flabbergasted smile and giddy eyes still resting on Eleanor. That was when I knew Chipper was in love.

He held her on a pedestal higher than baseball – higher than anything in the world! They talk about those girls who could stop a speeding train. Well, this one here stopped a ball game.

"Hey, Jennings! Tell your boy to step back in!"

Out came Jennings. "Hey, Doolin! What's the idea? You gotta – "

"She's here!"

"Who?"

"Eleanor. My, oh my! She came all the way to see me! Elly's here!"

"Aha! The special dame you take all the extra cuts for in battin' practice?"

"Yeah..."

"Hold on, Mac," said Jennings to the ump. "Listen, Doolin. Just hit it in the air – anywhere in the park. Just put it in the outfield n' do it for her n' give us a tie game. Got it?"

"Yeah..."

"Hey!"

"Y-yes, sir?"

"Let's go. You gotta hit. Take your eyes off her or Johnson's gonna paste a fastball right to your bee-hind. Your dame won't wanna date no guy with a lump in his rump."

"O-okay. That's right. I'll do good, sir!"

Doolin tipped his cap to Eleanor, who nodded with a poised and affectionate smile, but it was the wink of the eye that put Chip's soul in flight and all at once, he felt it. He felt the adrenaline creep through his young, vital body and his soul race to the tip of the world! It suddenly did not matter who was on the mound. Chip was filled with enough joy and confidence to hit that ball to the moon. He was in the big leagues and now he had a chance to be a hero in front of Eleanor.

He heard the noise of the crowd. He felt his legs, like poles of power as they moved back into the box. He saw the dirt fly as he dug his spikes into the ground. He thought of Eleanor. Nothing but Eleanor.

The pitch came and Chip Doolin connected – a long, deep, billowing drive to dead centerfield. Milan was on his horse, giving chase. He ran and ran until he ran out of room. In desperate measure, he leapt high above the fence, his glove outstretched to try and snare the ball, but it sailed over his glove *and* over the fence – Home run! Doolin put the Tigers on top, 4-2. As he crossed home plate, his teammates rushed to congratulate him. They were all in awe over the distance of the home run.

"That dame o' yours is comin' to every darn game she can! You got it!" said Jennings, a wry smile on his face.

"Yes, sir!"

"Way to go, Doolin! You gave me more than a tie

game. That was the longest ball I've seen hit in a long time – almost as long as Pennsylvania Avenue!"

The Tigers went on to preserve their 4-2 lead and win the season opener, disappointing a full Washington house, and this was how Chip Doolin's baseball career began, with a tip of his cap and a wink from the woman he adored, his heroics marked the beginning of baseball stardom.

A Bat Named, "Lucky"

*It is often the case:
Threaten a man's livelihood,
expect fury in return.*

Rumors were swirling around Michigan that the *Detroit Tiger* ball club was up for sale. The Tigers were the pride of Michigan, and rumors such as these were enough to cause a great stir amongst the people – which they did. In fact, the rumors resulted in an anxious mob collecting outside of the home of Frank J. Navin, the team owner, who was more surprised to hear the rumors than any other Detroit citizen, and he quickly tried to suppress them, fully aware that the people of Michigan felt they deserved to have a say in any transaction that involved *their* Tigers.

"I have not been approached by any person or group of people expressing interest in the ball club. These reports are unfounded. The Detroit Tigers are *not* for sale. I am the sole owner and I intend to keep it that way," said Navin, in a statement meant for the Detroit faithful.

It was soon learned, following an investigation by hired detectives – detectives hired by Navin himself – that the rumors were started by a few less-than-prestigious Boston businessmen whose business "connections" extended across the nation; men whose interest in baseball only went as far as their greed for money and control. The rumors had a purpose. They were meant to create a distraction, which they did, and designed to gauge or measure the very reaction to them. It was sheer trickery by a group of men known to the general public as *gangsters*, who had a knack for using pistols and muscle as their tools of persuasion.

Clandestine dealings lurked behind the scenes, in dark corners, secret alleys and pale, empty rooms. The Detroit players and their fans, from time to time, saw strange men in dark coats and wide-brimmed hats roaming the stands or slipping notes to reporters. Stories in the Detroit newspapers persisted, feeding the rumors and keeping them alive, and after a while, the fans wondered if there *was* any truth to them after all. Would there be an effort by the phantom group to buy – or worse, takeover their beloved Tigers?

"That's a whole lot o' bad dope them papers are reportin'," said Detroit manager Hughie Jennings.

Meanwhile, the Detroit Tiger baseball team did not seem to be distracted at all. Despite the rumors, they continued on a torrid pace, reeling off victory after victory, solidifying their place atop the standings as the first full quarter of the 1909 season unfolded; high Tiger batting averages and a stingy pitching staff made them the talk of the league.

Ty Cobb was leading the world in batting, with a .410 mark, and he already had twenty base swipes to compliment his early season feats. Donie Bush was leading the circuit in walks and Sam Crawford was tied for the lead in triples. Pitchers George Mullin and Ed Willett were battling each other for the lead in wins, both ahead of men with names like Bender, Plank, Joss, Johnson, Walsh, Waddell and Young. However, the player enjoying the most early season success was rookie first baseman, Chip Doolin. He was on fire!

Through twenty-two games, Doolin was chasing Cobb with a robust .401 average. He led the league in doubles and in runs scored, but the two statistics that glowed the most, were his home run and RBI numbers.

In 1909, home runs were hard to achieve; a scarcity to witness. Home run hitters were rare. High mounds and distant fences gave the game's advantage to the pitchers, but not when they faced Doolin.

NEAL D. BOGOSIAN

Chip's numbers were nothing short of astounding! Perhaps it was his boyish years in Virginia, hauling bales of hay or chopping wood or running reapers, or carrying baby boars and injured mares. Perhaps all of those thoughts of Eleanor and of Mama and Papa held the real secrets of the power behind that swing. Maybe it was the broomstick and those hard, harsh crab apples that were perishable rejects to most, but ripe baseballs in the eyes of Chip Doolin.

Since the turn of the century, the most home runs hit in both leagues, was just sixteen. It was done twice. In 1901, it was accomplished by Detroit's own, Sam Crawford, when he was with Cincinnati. In 1902, it was Socks Seybold of Philadelphia who achieved the same number. In 1909, through those first twenty-two games, Chip Doolin had already hit twelve – all with the same bat. His RBI total stood at forty. To the fans of Detroit, he was a spectacle, but to the fans and players in the rest of the league, he was a marvel. Some came to see Cobb. Others came to see Crawford or Mullin or Bush – but they *all* came to see the prized rookie, Doolin; he simply filled the house.

During one easy afternoon, just before another game under the sun, there was a hard knock on the door of Chip's room.

"Who could that be?" he said aloud.

When Chip opened the door, two burly men, in

long, dark coats and tilted, wide-brimmed fedoras, greeted him.

"Doolin, we need to talk," said one of the men, his words coming out very slowly and deliberately. He had a pock-marked face and a pudgy nose.

The men invited themselves into Chip's room and cornered him.

"What do you need to talk to me about?" asked Chip.

"We can make you a rich man, you see."

"I don't know what I'm supposed to see, but I think I seen you fellas around. Yes, I reckon I have," said Chip.

"Maybe you have," scoffed the pudge-nosed man, "and maybe you've been snoopin' in places you shouldn't."

"Snoop? I reckon I don't snoop. I seen you fellas 'round the dugout! That's where I seen you! What are your names?"

"I'm Paulie and this here..." he said, pointing a finger, "this is Crusher." Paulie's nose was so pudgy it looked like it was unrelated to a human body – as if it was some mutant that was orphaned and found residence on the face of the gangster, with a mind and body all its own. Besides his unsightly nose, Paulie's face was so marked it looked like a dart board.

"Crusher? What kind of a name is Crusher?" said Chip.

"Hey! What's with all the questions?" said Paulie. "We ask the questions, not you, but I don't think you want to find out why his name is Crusher. Now listen here, Doolin, and listen good...we like you. You're the best damn ballplayer on earth right now, and we can make you a rich man."

"How?"

"All you have to do is swing n' miss for a few weeks."

"Huh?"

"You got cotton in that head o' yours? Go out and swing n' miss a few is what I say," said Paulie.

"What the doggone you mean, 'swing n'miss'? I don't wanna be no 'swing n'miss' ballplayer – "

"But we do. You ballplayers aren't too bright are ya? Let me lay it out this way, real nice. Either you start strikin' out and stop hittin' those homers, or we're gonna fix you up real bad, you see? *Real* bad. Now let me say it like this, Doolin: You rub against money long enough, you come to want more of it. We can give you more of it," said Paulie, before dropping an envelope filled with cash on his chair. "Now we'll leave and you start missin' them balls – "

"No! Now you fellas take back this here package before you go and leave this here room, and you doggone better do it right fast!" The young Doolin pumped his chest out, showing his brawn, but inside he was growing nervous.

"Fine, Chipper. Have it your way. We'll leave like you say, but we'll just take your bat, along with this here package of dough like you say."

Crusher, who donned an angular, shadowy face with dark half-moons under his eyes, grabbed the bat that was leaning against the wall.

"Hey! You can't have that! You put it down right now or else!"

"'Or else' what, Chip? What are you gonna do? You're just a silly ballplayer. You ain't too bright are you? All we want you to do is go into a little slump for a while, you see? Or maybe when Crusher gets through with you, you may never swing a bat again, or maybe never walk onto another field," said Paulie. "You strikeout and me and my boys buy this club. Then we'll give you the fattest contract in the game. It's that simple. Whatta you say?"

"Give Lucky back to me…now!" said Chip, his innards beginning to seethe with mounting anger and his face turning red as fire.

"Okay, Chip. Have it your way. We'll see ya." Crusher seized the bat and the two gangsters went for the door.

Chip flexed and lunged after the two men. His country muscle lifted the pock-marked wise guy and threw him across the room, in one fluid motion. Then he grabbed the throat of Crusher. It was a ferocious grip, that must have drained the last breath of life from the gangster's soul, because he dropped the bat and fell to the floor.

Chip was stunned over what he had just done – what had suddenly come over him. I remember it took him a few days to get over it. His instant anger was a revelation, as if coming on at the flip of a switch. He never knew he was capable of such intense emotion and action, and it scared him.

After Chip got his bat back, he replaced it gently against the wall, next to the door.

As he carried Crusher to the other side of the room, the bat boy slipped in unseen, grabbed the bat and closed the door. He was making his daily rounds before game time, collecting the bats of all the players, bringing them down to the field and putting them neatly in the bat rack.

Pudge-nose Paulie was the first to come back to his senses.

"What are you going to do with us? I've got all the money – "

"Well," said Chip, interrupting him, "first I'm gonna call the police. Both you men trespassed here, braabed me and tried to steal me, and I know trespassin' is 'gainst the law cuz I remember when someone tried to steal my Papa's cow. My Papa said he was trespassin' n' walkin' where he ain't suppose to, and so Papa shot him in the but-tocks. I ain't got my gun with me now...so I'm gonna get the police," finished Chip. He turned toward the door. "Lucky!" Chip turned back around and glared at the two gangsters.

"We didn't take it! We didn't take it!" cried Paulie.

"Did you fellas send someone else up to take Lucky?" asked Chip, with blood the color of anger rushing through his face again. "WAS ANOTHER ONE O' YOU STANDIN' OUTSIDE THAT DOOR, CUZ I'LL – "

"NO! NO!" they screamed.

Then there was another knock at the door. Chip rushed to its handle and flung it open. It was the building manager.

"Say, what's all the commotion about, Chip? By golly, it's almost game time!"

"Mr. Manager, sir...I seem to have lost – have you seen, Lucky?"

"Who?"

"Lucky, my bat?"

"God! No, Chip. I'm sorry, I sure haven't – "

"I want you to call the police n' have these two fellas arrested for trespassin' n' for batnappin' n' braab – I mean, braabry."

"You mean, 'bribery'?"

"Yes! I gotta go find Lucky. I think these men mighta took it somehow," said Chip.

"Chip, you ought to get down to the field. You

better go right now. They'll have a bat for you until you find your own. Now don't you worry about a thing. You don't want to miss the game do you?"

"No, sir."

"Then you best be going right now. You got less than twenty-five minutes. By the looks of them these boys aren't going anywhere fast."

Chip hurried down to the street and ran the three blocks that led to Bennett Park.

He pulled his cap down low and in street clothes, rushed his way through the crowd. The stands were filling fast with people who were there to see Chip and the rest of the Tigers play the Boston Red Sox.

He entered the locker room dejected and sad and when he did, his teammates rushed to his side.

"Chip! Hey Chip what's wrong? What is it, boy? Where ya been?"

"Where ya been, Chip?" asked manager Jennings. "You had us all worried. You got Eleanor all nervous. She thinks you mighta – say! What's wrong Chipper? Why the long face?"

"Yeah, Chipper. What's wrong? You can tell us," prodded Donie Bush.

"I'm sorry fellas. I can't find Lucky and I think two bribers done me in – "

"Lucky's right there, Chip! Right in the rack where the boy put it!" exclaimed Jennings, pointing to the bat rack. "Don't you remember? He goes 'round and gets'em every day!"

Chip looked at the bat rack and the heavy worry in his eyes disappeared. He saw the knob of the bat that he painted red. "Lucky! It's you!" He leaped like a boy on a springboard. He grabbed the bat and kissed the barrel, "Aww, fellas...I'm mighty sorry for scarin' y'all...I must o' lost my head with all that just went on."

Chip spent the next five minutes telling his friends all about Pudge Nose Paulie and Crusher.

Not long after, two exciting syllables rang through the park, "Play ball!"

Chip Doolin went four-for-four and celebrated the recovery of Lucky with home runs number thirteen and fourteen off Boston hurler Eddie Cicotte, en route to another Tiger win.

The gangsters were arrested and thrown behind bars – and all of the rumors disappeared with them.

The Detroit club, mysteriously, was no longer for sale.

W-W-Would You M-M-Marry Me?

The breath of love is an affliction. Like an illness, it is not easy to resist once it strikes. True love is an investment of the heart; a time when the heart, mind and soul are all tied up in the same place and thoughts are of nothing else, but the fresh pull at the deepest part of you.

It was game day when the blustery New England winds swept and swirled the infield dirt at Huntington Park, home of the *Boston Red Sox*. It was a morning in which Chip Doolin rose earlier than normal, stirring in restless anticipation of the eventful day ahead. His boyish excitement gripped him in the same way he had already gripped the national baseball faithful, who had faith that Chip could launch a home run every time he stepped to the plate.

Those New England winds seemed to be blowing in a different fashion on this day, rustling something fateful in their might. All the night prior Chip tossed and turned, his mind churning and churning, weighted heavily by love and one of the most important impending moments of his young life. The knot that persisted in his stomach jettisoned any hopes for a restful night's sleep.

As soon as the hues from the rising sun illuminated his room, Chip was up and out of bed. He bathed and dressed amidst his scattered thoughts, not giving full attention to the actual processes of "bathing" and "dressing" – and with traces of shave cream still under his nose and ears, and wearing a pair of odd-colored socks – one red and one blue – he went and knocked on Donie Bush's hotel room door.

"Ty said we should get up early," said Chip from the other side of the door.

"He didn't mean before the dang birds sing, Chip!" yelled Donie from his bed.

"Okay, I'll go get me some breakfast downstairs. I'll buy a paper n' have a look at some o' them adver-tizements so we'll know just where to go."

"Yeah, you go do that Chip...good idea, now that you sprung me from the swell dreams I was havin' – dreamin' o' hittin' .400 which'll never happen in this here reality," said Bush.

Chip went downstairs and had a double order of eggs, ham and toast, while he scanned the paper as best he could, skipping the "big words" in the newsprint. Over the years, I had a lot to do with expanding Chip's education and his vocabulary. He always wanted to know the meaning of words that were foreign to him. When he was a rookie, it seemed almost *every* word was foreign to him.

Later that morning, he was scheduled to be at Boston's City Hall, where he was to be honored and presented with a key to the city, his reward for putting a ring of hoodlums behind bars. The hoodlums were the same boys who tried to strong-arm their way into buying the Detroit franchise, and bribe Chip into "swinging n' missing a few".

Following the ceremony at City Hall, Ty Cobb, Sam Crawford and Donie Bush, were to accompany Chip to some Boston jewelry shops, to help him find a ring; Chip was convinced that he wanted Eleanor to be his wife and lifetime companion, and he decided it was apt time to propose. In actuality, the question of whether to propose was decided for Chip much earlier – a young boy's crush on a young girl; a hometown love that lasted through teen years and on into adulthood…with a friendship that is rare between two people, still pure and untainted. Chip was comforted in knowing that Eleanor was someone who understood him. He felt safe around her, finding safety in the thought that they came from the same place, on those two neighboring farms in Somewhere, Virginia, and he always remembered what she would say to him as they lay on their backs during idle hours, staring at the great blue sky over them, lying long ways, the tips of their heads touching, "Well, Chip...don't ever forget your closest friends from your childhood. They will be the only ones in your life who will always know where you came from – especially when you get old."

"Yeah," Chip would reply, "my Mama tells me that good friends are like cherry blossoms, but they never stop blossomin'! She says they always bloomin' n' such, n' I tell her that I never see any flowers growin' 'round my friend's ears."

I remember Chip telling me how nervous he was, how his head was racing and as those of us who have ever been in love know, love carries with it a euphoria that can make one dizzy with affection; from the top of the head to the tips of the toes, a euphoria that intoxicates and infects, injecting an extra pep in your step, feeling as though at any moment you might take flight to the skies.

⚾ ⚾ ⚾

Amongst all of the priorities pressing his mind, Chip could not forget, most of all, the Tiger's mid-afternoon divisional clash against 'Smokey' Joe Wood and the temperamental Red Sox.

He was glad to find Cobb and Crawford up and

about when he knocked on their door.

"Hey, Chip! Been up since six," said Ty Cobb, "had to oil the glove. C'mon in. Sam's readin' the paper."

"Hiya Chipper!" exclaimed 'Wahoo' Sam Crawford. "Philly won again – looks like it's gonna be a close one this year. A fight to the finish and – " he paused to look Chip over, "you just can't wait can ya? You're as fidgety as a hog in heat!"

"Darn it, Sam, why I'm – I'm...I'm so darn excited, Sam! I could throw a baseball from here to Iowa n' I'd still nail the chicken to the barn! I can't wait to see Eleanor's face when I give it to her, and tell her all the rest I wanna do for her, but my blood's pumpin' so dang fast I can't remember what the rest is – "

"Chip, slow down. You have to ask'er first before you give *anything* to her," advised Cobb. "You mean you can't wait to see her *face* when you propose and the fine look – "

"Ahh, he don't give a hoot about the honor at City Hall. He only cares about his dame, and a mighty fine one she is."

"Thanks Sam, but I do care about the honor. Honest I do, but, but – "

"Your heart's all tied up n' singin' a fine tune – we know all about it," said Cobb.

"That's *just* what it feels like – " said Chip.

"Chipper, love is the only pure risk in life. That's why it's such a thrill," said Crawford. "Sometimes you win the risk and sometimes you lose, and when you lose, you never forget the feel of that heartache as long as you live – but I think you're a winner in this here affair."

"Where'd ya read that, Sammy?" asked Cobb.

"Well..."

"Oh, no! Don't tell me you thought o' that yourself!"

"Alright! Geez, Ty...can't you let me have one of'em? I read some of it in *Harper's* an some I sure have knowed myself."

"See, Chip? I get'em every time."

At 9:00 all four ballplayers were in the lobby, donned in pressed suits and ready to go to the ceremony.

By 9:45 Chip Doolin was on a wooden stage, sitting on a wooden chair and smiling politely while Boston's Mayor, George Hibbard, read his prepared words of honor:

> "...and when the notorious "Pudge Nose" Paulie tried to bully him into throwing his own game, well...Chip

Doolin would have none of it and he made his stance known. And when they tried to steal his favorite bat that he calls, 'Lucky', in an act of blackmail, Chip flexed some muscle and heroically out-muscled the two thugs and piled them in a corner. Chip not only performed a service for this city but for the entire country, including the people and fans of his own Detroit. I proudly present this key to the best first bagger in the league – Chip Doolin!"

But when Chip got up from the wooden chair, the seat of his twill pants got caught on a protruding nail. His pants ripped from his thigh right down to his ankle, revealing his white knickers. The luminaries on stage were in dismay, but fortunately the mishap went unnoticed by the crowd, drowned by their own thunderous applause upon his introduction. Chip quickly sought refuge behind the podium, where he was able to hide his exposed right leg. However, the mayor's secretary seated behind Chip got a full view of his white under shorts.

The police chief alertly grabbed his overcoat and with a smile, put it over Chip's shoulders and promptly took off his badge and put it on the lapel of the coat, further improvising and making it part of the honor.

Chip nodded awkwardly and managed to crack an embarrassing smile, which the crowd perceived as his admirable trait of humbleness.

With his face beet red and his body riddled with the shakes, Chip didn't give much in the way of a speech. In fact, he barely said anything at all.

"Thank you," he gushed, trying to gather his senses. A cool seasonal breeze blew across the crowd and found its way beneath Chip's new overcoat, flapping it open – he quickly shut it. "I'm honored and – and grateful to have this..." and he remembered what Cobb told him to say, "this is a wonderful city and I will always look forward to returning," and then he added, "especially now that I have a key to get me in." Chip finished with a wave to the applauding crowd, before stepping out from behind the podium.

The Police Chief let him keep the coat to always remember the occasion and when he got off the stage, he told the rest of the boys about the blunder.

"So we need to get you some new britches," said Donie Bush. "That tear is big enough to hide a baby."

"Yeah, Chip, you need some britches before we go look for a ring," said Cobb, "or the jewelers will think you're tryin' to woo'em or somethin' funny to get a good bargain, showin' that leg off n' such."

THE ADVENTURES OF CHIP DOOLIN

"Aw, shucks! That darn nail!"

"No sweat, Chip. There are plenty o' shops right in Copley Square."

The first jeweler they happened on was as useless as a paper baseball bat. There was not any inventory in his display cases – no rings or watches or jewelry of any kind, anywhere.

"Tell me what you like. Tell me what you want. I order for you," said the merchant, in a thick Armenian accent.

"No, we need something we can see," said Cobb.

"Oh, nonsense. You can see in your imagination, and then tell me what you see."

"No thanks," said Bush.

"Yes! Yes!" said the merchant.

"No! No! No!" said Bush.

"You foolish Americans. I can get you big, big shiny stone!"

"Yeah, prob'ly from the coal mine," said Crawford, before the four men walked out of the shop.

They then came upon a small, private-looking store that seemed to have a certain charm hovering around its doorstep. They went in hoping it had something to match Chip's romantic endeavors.

As soon as they walked in a wiry salesman greeted them. He had a long, sloping nose and two sets of crooked fingers that had been afflicted with hard work.

"Step right up, my boy! You're the lucky man, are you? Well have I got something for you!"

"Sir, he would like – "

"That's right, you boys just sit over there. Have I got something for you, young man? I sure do! What's your name?"

"Uh, my name is – "

"What's that? What'd you say?"

"Chip. His name is Chip."

"And I told you to sit down!" he said to the humbled Sam Crawford. "How's the boy gonna say 'I do' if he can't say his own name? Eh? Now what's your name son?"

"Chip."

"A chip off the old block, aye? Well have I got a ring for you – what's the girl's name?"

"Eleanor," said Chip with a dreamy smile.

"Oh, yes. This ring I'm going to show you has her name all over it. I believe you'll be able to see Eleanor deep in the corners of this stone, sitting patiently and waiting for you to slide it on her finger – and you'll see her smile in its sparkle!"

"I will?"

"You sure will, my boy."

"Now wait one minute," said Cobb.

"We'll wait for nothing. There's not a minute

to lose! Now you go back over there and sit or I'll throw you out of my shop!"

The salesman, who was the sole proprietor, momentarily disappeared behind a velvet curtain before returning with a solid gold engraved box – engraved and etched in Victorian royalty; mystical, multi-colored stones and jewels that conjured timeless wonders of love and romantic whispers, moonlight kisses and what remained of the breathy lust of ages past.

The man slowly placed the box before Chip. There was a spell of silence as he admired the beauty of it. Then the salesman said softly, "Okay, Chipper. Now open it."

When Chip opened the cover of the box, he gasped; his reaction spurred Cobb, Crawford and Bush to scurry to their feet and look over Chip's shoulder. When they did, they also gasped in awe, struck by the luminous and stately aura of the ring.

"Didn't I say I had something?" said the proprietor, calmness and wisdom coloring his voice.

"That's the one! That's Eleanor! You were right, sir. This would look mighty fine n' pretty on her finger. I want it."

"I had a friend. This was his great-grandmother's ring, going back to the early 1800's. She lived in London. You look and act a lot like he did – innocent. Give me two hundred and it's yours."

Chip reached into his pocket and handed over the money, and the three-carat cluster ring adorned with rubies, was his to give.

"Hey boys, we better be headin' back, we're gonna be late," said Cobb.

"Yeah, boys," began the proprietor, "you better be getting back to the ballpark, you've got a big game against Smokey Joe. He's a tough one and I have never seen anyone run around in centerfield like that Tris Speaker fellow. Kind chap, too!"

The boys could only look at each other in surprise.

"You recognize us?" said Crawford.

"You all think I don't follow the game? It has been a pleasure meeting you, Chip Doolin. I've heard a lot about you."

He extended his hand to Chip.

"Thank you, sir."

"It has been an honor to serve you – Hey! Would you all mind signing a ball for me before you go? I have it right here – " said the proprietor, reaching behind the counter.

"It would be our pleasure, sir," said Chip.

"Good! And then go and get some hits for me – and you Chip, try and hit a long one. And you, Mr. Cobb, try not to steal so many doggone bases," he said smiling. "I'll look forward to reading about you boys in the paper."

THE ADVENTURES OF CHIP DOOLIN

They got outside and hailed a horse-drawn taxi.

Donie Bush was the last to step up into the cab and when he did, he lost his footing and fell badly on his ankle.

"Oh, no! The skipper won't like this!" said Chip.

Some time was lost tending to Bush before the horse and buggy raced to the ballpark as fast as it could. They arrived only twenty minutes before the game's first pitch.

Chip walked into the clubhouse with an oversized wooden key cradled in his arms. Donie Bush came in behind him, helped by Cobb and Crawford on either side. Bush was favoring his bad ankle, limping badly.

"Hi, boys! Nice of you to make it!" said Hughie Jennings, the Tiger skipper.

It was determined that Bush had a sprained ankle, and when the game started, Charley O'Leary was the starting shortstop, taking his place in the lineup.

The game was tied 0–0 going into the ninth, as Ed Willett dueled Joe Wood to the very end; pitch for pitch, the hurlers gave Boston fans a real clinic in the art of pitching.

Willett had yielded just two hits to Wood's three. Harry Hooper and Tris Speaker owned the hits for the Red Sox while Ty Cobb, Germany Schaefer and Chip, each had one for the Tigers.

Wood started the ninth in usual style, whiffing George Moriarty and Sam Crawford, before Chip came up. He remembered the proprietor's request to hit a long one, and he swung at the first pitch he saw from Wood, making contact and sending the ball to straight away left – but it looked to be only an opposite-field fly ball, when all of a sudden those New England winds stirred and swept across the field. It was one of the craziest things I ever did see. Those mighty gusts grabbed the ball and carried it further, deeper. Boston's left fielder Hooper was suddenly sprinting for the fences, trying to track the ball. Back he went, racing against the swirling spring winds, chasing it all the way to the fences. The flavors of fate and victory must have indeed been in those winds, because that ball kept carrying right over the fence! Only when the ball sailed out of reach, did the winds calm and Chip Doolin rounded the bases for his fourteenth home run of the season. It made the Tigers 1-0 winners, as Willett retired the Red Sox in order in the bottom of the ninth. I think that was when the notion first occurred to me, that the God or Gods that rule the earth – whatever your faith – really must have liked Chipper.

Chip's wind-swept home run made headlines, but all he could think of was getting back to Detroit to give the ring to Eleanor – nothing else mattered as much to him.

THE ADVENTURES OF CHIP DOOLIN

He met her at the train. She was the picture of elegance in a long, crème-colored dress. It matched well with her rich blonde hair and the most fascinating curls that ever fell over a woman's face – Eleanor was certainly a keeper, always well-groomed, polite and the best taste in everything, right down to her manicured nails and lipsticked smile, but on this occasion, nestled into her hair, was a sprig of cherry blossoms.

"Gee, Elly...it's you! *You're* my closest friend! You're blossomin' n' bloomin' all over!"

From the station they went to dinner. Chip reserved a booth in one of Detroit's finest restaurants. He was a bundle of nerves that night, shaking all over, because his heart was fluttering giddily with love.

Chip knew he had to pop the question early, or he would never be able to eat, let alone order his food. In fact, Chip's thoughts were in such a flux that when they sat down, he ordered a cracker instead of a cola.

"A cracker?" said the waiter.

"Y-yes."

"Just one?"

"Well, I reckon I can't drink two at once."

"Mr. Doolin, sir, you can't drink a cracker unless

that's a drink I've not heard of – "

"No, he meant, "cola" not "cracker"," said Eleanor, who turned to Chip, tenderly grabbing his arm and said, "Dear, you ordered a cracker."

"Oh, well, m-maybe bring me some soup with it if that's what you're sellin'."

"Sir?"

"We'll have just the two drinks for now, thank you," said Eleanor to the waiter.

Chip feared his inability to say the 'M – ' word, and so, he figured that maybe if he practiced some words that started with 'm', he might be able to gain enough confidence to say the word he wanted to say.

"Elly, do you like them m-m-mina-ture poodle dogs?"

"Well, I'm not sure – "

"Well cuz I was thinkin' about dogs, that's all – what about m-m-marigolds, Elly? Them flowers? Do you like'em?"

"I suppose I do, yes – "

"And w-what about m-m-mys-tree novels? My Papa likes to listen to'em when my Mama reads'em."

"I haven't really read a good one, I don't think. I like Charles Dickens and Jane Austen – "

"What about math-a-matics? One o' the umpires I know sure is a whiz at it, 'specially countin' all them balls n' strikes. And Elly, do you believe in m-miracles?"

"Yes I do, but I'm not very good at math – "

"Okay Elly, umm...okay...one more," said Chip, shifting in his seat. Perspiration began to swell on his forehead and drip from his armpits. His palms were moist and his face was a nervous and pallid white, "Uh, what about – "

"Chipper?"

"Yes, Elly?"

"Honey, calm down, take a deep breath – "

"Aww shucks, Elly. I'm gonna run outta the breath I got if I don't get this out – what about m-m-m-m-marriage? Doggone it, Elly!" said Chip, slamming his fist on the table, "W-w-would you – "

"Yes! Yes! Yes!"

"You will? But you don't know what you're yes-sin' to!"

"Yes, Chip Doolin, you adorable man, I'll marry you!"

Chip reached into his pocket and pulled out the diamond ring, "I – I almost forgot," he said, fumbling with it in his hand.

The Boston merchant was right. The ring was all about Eleanor...her smile was in its sparkle; her name, their love, it was all snuggled deep in its depths.

The Swing That Got Him There

It was a cool, easy spring in 1909, and when the baseball season ripened, the Tigers were still in first place. I remember when they faced-off with the fourth place New York Highlanders that season, because Chipper found himself mired in the first slump of his big league career.

"Don't think too much about it Chip, n' stop tryin' to tinker with your stance. I think you're just swingin' underneath the ball – you've lowered your hands," advised Sam Crawford, "get'em back up above your shoulders."

The psychology of a ballplayer – the psychology of baseball, can be a harrowing dilemma, especially for a country farm boy like Doolin. The game itself is a delicate case study, bound in superstitions and habit, and strung up in nerves that are wrung from the efforts of perfection.

When the bat is having difficulty finding the

ball, the ballplayer must resist the propensity for his struggles to drown his confidence, but when a sudden and untimely experience threatens to thwart the psyche even further, a myriad of negative possibilities are exposed – outcomes that could topple something that was once so promising, like a flourishing career. Doom can quickly bear down on a vulnerable psyche, especially a young one, preying on weakness. It quickly becomes an affliction on the afflicted, if but for a few long moments, and perhaps, dependant on the strength of the man, for the rest of time, erasing him into oblivion.

Chip had been slumping badly. He was entering the New York series with just three hits in the last two weeks, all singles – a span of thirteen games and forty-four plate appearances. His average had fallen from .398 to .342 and manager Jennings started to ponder whether he ought to give his young star a day off. With Chip's slump, the Tiger lead over second place Philadelphia had shrunk to just two games.

"Hey, Chipper, how do ya feel today?" asked Jennings.

"I feel okay. I'm tryin' mighty hard, sir."

"I know you are, Chip. Maybe you should let up a bit."

Chip was puzzled at the suggestion. "Let up?" he said.

"Sure, Chipper. Don't try so hard. Have faith in the swing that gotcha here."

Chip cocked his head to one side, considering the advice. He liked the sound of the phrase, "the swing that got me here," and he mumbled it to himself right up until game time.

Later that afternoon, five foot, nine-inch Jack Warhop took the mound for the Highlanders. The twenty-seven year old Warhop was not the imposing type, but he was gutsy and he knew how to pitch.

When the lineups were posted, Chip still had his third slot in the batting order.

Donie Bush, his first game back from an ankle sprain, was the first to face the lanky righthander, and first pitch swinging he hit a weak pop to short.

The next batter was Ty Cobb, who was in the midst of enjoying another fine season. He dug into the box and waited patiently, watching, "Ball One!" and then "Ball Two!" sail by, before promptly smacking the third pitch into left field for a base hit.

Chip eyed the field as he normally did when he walked to the batter's box. He took a deep breath and inhaled the fragrance of crisp, clean air, just the kind of air in which a ball can carry when it is well struck.

"C'mon, Chipper!" chanted Cobb from first.

Chip nodded, gripped the bat and stepped in. Warhop wound and threw.

"Strike One!" screamed the umpire. It was a fastball just above the knees.

Warhop climbed the mound again and stared in for the sign from catcher, Red Kleinow. He checked it, went into his wind-up and Cobb took off for second. The pitch came. Chip took a mighty cut at the ball and missed. Kleinow fired down to his second baseman Frank LaPorte, but it wasn't in time and Cobb was safe with a stolen base.

Doolin stepped out of the box and took another deep breath. The lack of confidence that is sibling to slumps started to crease onto his face. Chip smoothed the home plate dirt before digging back in. He waved his bat and waited.

Warhop got the sign and adjusted the ball in his glove. He looked Cobb back to the second base bag, and then he kicked and threw to the plate. The laces turned fast! It was a high, hard fastball and before young Doolin could react, the ball slammed into his head like a torpedo and rolled to the backstop. Doolin fell to the ground, as the gasping crowd rose to its feet.

Instead of racing for third, Cobb ran to home plate to check on his friend. The Tiger dugout emptied. Hughie Jennings was the first to reach him.

"Chip! Chip! Can ya hear me? Speak to me, pal."

Chip was slowly rolling his head from side to side.

"Hey, Chipper, can you open your eyes?" asked a concerned Germany Schaefer.

The bat boy came rushing out with a towel and first aid kit.

"Oh, he'll be fine. What are you boys so concerned for? It didn't even hit'em," squawked the umpire.

The Tiger players roared in protest.

"Hold on boys! Hold on!" said Jennings. "What the heck – whatta you mean it didn't hit'em? It most certainly did! What in the devil do you think the boy's on the ground for? He's sure not down there cuz he likes to kiss the dirt! Good God, look at'em!"

"Hey, Kleinow," said the ump, "did that ball hit Doolin?"

Kleinow stared out to Warhop and Kid Elberfeld, and wearing a blank face replied, "I didn't see nothin'."

"Why you dirty, no good rat!" snarled Cobb before starting after him, but the players managed to restrain Cobb. "He just don't want us to have another runner!"

"Umpire, that ball hit'em!" yelled Jennings.

"Kleinow said it didn't."

"That's cuz Kleinow's a blind man and he's up to no good – "

"I knew you needed glasses but now I think you

need new eyes! Or…are you too darn corrupt to call this game?" said Donie Bush to the umpire. "My grandpa coulda called it the right way if he was umpin' this game, even if he was standin' in the rains of England!"

"Say…who hired you for this contest? The league or the team?" asked Jennings.

"Watch it Jennings or I'll throw you outta the park and write the league!"

"Bein' so blind, how do ya expect to write?" replied Jennings.

By then, Chip's eyes were open and he was rubbing the welt on his head.

"C'mon, Chipper! Boys help him to the bench."

"He's got another strike!" said the umpire. "You gonna forfeit the out?"

"You can have it! Can't you see the boy's hurtin'? Look at the bruise on his skull. How'd that get there? I suppose he got that from restin' on a pillow. Why I ought to give you one just the same!"

"Watch it!"

"*You* watch it! What was your name? *Lyden* is it? They ought to call you, 'Lyden the Liar' and I'm gonna write the darn league about *you*! I'll take care of you!"

"Well, I didn't see no ball hit'em."

"That's cuz you're a blind liar! It hit'em I say and the whole park saw it! You know…" said Jennings, moving closer to the umpire, "my Papa used to quote a wise fellow named Bacon, who wrote, "To lie is to be brave before God and a dang coward toward man." You sure ain't brave, Lyden, and I'd say that coward part was written with the likes o' you in mind!"

Chip was now on his feet shaking everyone's hands away, "I can stand on my own. I'm mighty fine. Ain't no one gonna forfeit my out. I can hit."

"Chipper, I'd rather you seek some doctor attention."

"I don't need no doctor, I'm ready to hit."

"Can you see alright?"

"I can see you just fine."

"What about a ball, Chip?" asked Sam Crawford. "Can you see this?" And he tossed it to Matty McIntyre, the Tiger left fielder.

"I can see it just fine. This here umpire says it didn't hit me n' that's just fine. He must be rootin' for the other team n' I'm gonna make'em wish he didn't."

With reluctance, the Tiger team relented and left Chip to hit.

Cobb went back to second base. Warhop took the mound. Kleinow crouched behind the plate and the umpire got set behind him. Applause rang through the stands.

Chip loosened some kinks in his neck before

standing tall and looking out across the field. He looked down the barrel of his bat, and then he remembered, *Keep my hands up. The swing that got me here.* He peered into the Tiger dugout and tipped his cap to Hughie Jennings.

"Doolin just tipped his cap to me," said Jennings in the dugout. "I'll bet anyone ten bucks he hits one to the moon in this here at bat."

There were no takers on Jennings' challenge.

"Play ball!" shouted the umpire. "Let's go Doolin!"

"You got a loud mouth, Mr. Umpire. You ought to be in them Vaude-ville shows r' somethin'. I'll go awlright. Just the same, I'm gonna watch you go get this here ball after I hit it," said a defiant Chip.

"What'd you say?" said the umpire.

"Nothin'. Let's go."

Chip stepped into the box, raised his hands above his shoulder, rocked the bat back and forth, and waited to unleash his anger on the next pitch.

Warhop wound and dealt.

Chip swung and got a piece of it – a foul tip that went off his bat and ricocheted off the arm of the umpire, who winced in pain.

"You okay, ump?" asked Red Kleinow.

Jeers, claps and laughter came from the Tiger dugout, "How's it feel?" and "What comes around goes around," were the phrases that I remember, along with a few words not fit for repeating on these pages, but I jotted them down and recorded the whole scene in my notes.

Embarrassed and bitter the ump snapped, "Let's go, Doolin! Get back in there! I'll get you yet!"

"But I ain't done nothin' to you, Mr. Umpire."

There was a brief pause before the umpire replied, "Oh, let's go...! *Let's go*, I said, get in the box."

I think that umpire was actually jealous of Chip, but jealousy is like a germ, sooner or later it will get you, and boy did it get umpire Lyden. Cobb danced off second. Warhop stared in to check the sign. Chip watched the pitcher wind and throw. And then as if in slow motion, like days before the slump, he saw the ball as clear as the shiny blue sky; he read the rotation of the seams, knowing how it would fall. He cocked and swung. The crowd let out an exclamation at the solid sound of the ball connecting with the bat.

Home run number fifteen did not take long to leave the park. It looked like a lead pellet that was shot from a canon.

Three more doubles in his next three at-bats knocked Chip out of his slump for good, and propelled the Tigers to an 8–0 drubbing over their divisional foes.

"You sure are a competitor, Chipper!" said Jennings after the game. "A dandy of a competitor are you, and you got one hard head."

I learned something new about Chip's determination that day, and what kind of a man he really was. I think he surprised everyone, even Jennings.

It was that one strike he took back that broke his slump…and the event fortified his reputation even further.

From the Rivers of Youth

Tyler Shannon ran into his father's work den bursting with energy. It was early morning, but the sun was already as strong as if it were midday, dousing the den with its bright, effervescent rays. Tyler loved visiting his father in his den. It made him feel as though he was entering into a completely separate structure disconnected from his house – a whole other existence; an office in a bustling city surrounded by skyscrapers, where plans were drawn up to save the world from invaders; a work station in a clandestine location overseas, where spy exercises were regularly conducted; at night it became an underground vestibule where top secret activity transpired. It was all the product of Tyler's active imagination and youthful concoctions, the kind of imagination not at all strange to young boys. On this day, his energy and excitement stemmed from something more…he was going to a ball game.

"Daddy! Daddy! Can we go early and get some

of the ballplayers to write their names on my ball?"

"We sure can, Tyler, but under one condition...."

"Okay."

"You have to promise me that you won't forget to take your medicine before we leave."

"Okay, I promise. That's an easy one, Daddy."

"Well, we don't want your mother to be mad at us do we?"

"No, Daddy, that's not fun when Mommy's mad at us, she makes that funny face."

"That's my boy!"

"Do you think I'll get to meet Chip Doolin?"

"If we get there early enough I don't see why you shouldn't. He seems nice enough to – "

"And Ty Cobb too, Daddy!" His eyes were widening and the excitement rose through his shoulders.

Tyler was just seven summers old and barely over four feet tall. That afternoon he had a date at the Detroit ballpark, where the Tigers would battle Rube Waddell and the St. Louis Browns.

"We'll see what we can do. Now run upstairs and straighten your room so when the time comes to leave, we won't be delayed," said his father.

"Okay, Daddy!"

And little Tyler was quickly off, scurrying up the stairs. The *Detroit Tigers* were his favorite team, and Chip Doolin was his all-time hero. At night, baseball was part of his every dream. His bedroom was adorned with Tiger pennants, team pictures, baseball cards and newspaper clippings featuring Chip and his monumental baseball feats. Tyler would spend long intervals just staring at his collection, while throwing a baseball into his glove. He'd simulate baseball games and suddenly insert himself as the starting left fielder that made the diving catch, or the fireball pitcher who won the big game. Once in a while he would get so taken up in his own imagination, that he'd check the newspaper the next morning to see if any of it really *did* happen – if his nine inning shutout *did* occur or his home run ball that landed in Lake Michigan really *was* found by a fisherman who just happened to catch the fish that caught the ball. He'd practice swinging his bat like Chip Doolin swung, and he'd lead off of first base the way Cobb did, just before he stole second.

Tyler couldn't wait to go see the Tigers play the Browns that day; it was his chance to see all of his fantasies unfold.

⚾ ⚾ ⚾

The freshness of folly greeted Tyler and his father when they got their tickets at the ticket gate. Spirits were lofty amongst the fans that lined up at the turnstile, waiting to enter the park.

"Do you smell that, Tyler? Do you smell it?"

"Yeah, Daddy, I can smell the grass and – " and Tyler began coughing, an uncontrollable, heaving chest cough that overcame him and riddled his young frame, crippling his capacity to even stand up straight. His father quickly undid the straps of the knap sack he had slung around his shoulder and pulled out a canteen of water.

"Drink some water, Tyler. C'mon, buddy."

Spectators and fans alike continued to move into the ballpark in swarms, passing them on the left and right, all but enveloping Mr. Shannon, as he tended to his son.

"Did you take your medicine like you were supposed to?"

"No, Daddy. I'm sorry that I always forget."

"It's okay little buddy, you're lucky I brought it with me."

Tyler's face went from a frown to a smile. "Mommy can't get mad at us now!"

Frank Shannon, Tyler's dad, was a friend of mine. He was a ballplayer himself, who played in the Big Leagues for the Washington Senators and Louisville Colonels, but his stint was short-lived, and he hit just .160 in thirty-two career games. Nonetheless, little Tyler was proud of his Daddy's one-time professional status and he never failed to brag about it to all of his friends.

As they descended toward the field, Tyler spotted

a familiar face. "There he is, Daddy! There's Mr. Doolin! He's signing for those people!"

They hurried down to the railing, but as they did, Chip was pulled away from the crowd to take part in infield warm-ups.

Disappointed but hopeful, father and son settled into the nearby box seats.

It was a fine day to play ball. The sun was shining and the smells of leather and wood and grass filled the air. Starry, young eyes glistened throughout the park – young fans who got a first-hand look at their baseball heroes.

I always got a real kick out of watching those youngsters. I always said that our human civilization could learn a lot from studying all the little people in the world. They are the closest to perfection that we will ever be, still undaunted, uncorrupted and innocent.

Anyway, fans everywhere in the park were there to consume popcorn, peanuts and baseball, symbols of the American way, and they all tipped their hats to the flag hoisted in centerfield, before taking their seats.

When infield warm-ups were finished, it was Tyler's Dad who exclaimed, "Excuse me, Mr. Doolin! Would you be kind enough to sign my boy's ball?"

Tyler was not able to yell because of the soreness in his throat and the malady in his lungs. Chip, the full-fledged pro and role model to countless youngsters, heard the request and without hesitation, walked over to Mr. Shannon with a smile.

"Hi, I'm Chip Doolin. It's a mighty pleasure to meet you, sir."

"Hello, I'm Frank Shannon and I'd like you to meet my son, Tyler."

"Hi, Tyler. It's mighty nice to meet you," said Chip, extending his hand.

"H-h-hello, M-Mr. Doolin," said Tyler in a low, raspy voice.

"I'd be happy to sign the ball you got there."

"Okay..."

"Thank you, Chip. Congratulations on the fine season you're having," said Mr. Shannon.

"Thank you. I'm just honored to help out this here team n' try to keep us in first place."

Chip's inscription on the ball read: *Best Wishes, Chip Doolin.* When he handed it back to Tyler, the starstruck boy was unresponsive, his awe having settled in his mouth.

"Thank you so much, Chip," said Frank Shannon, answering for his son.

"Where ya'll sittin'?"

"Just over there."

"Oh, those are mighty fine seats. Can't get much better than the front row. I hope ya'll enjoy the game n' it was great meetin' you, Tyler."

"Y-you too, Mr. Doolin," and just as Chip turned to walk away, Tyler summoned enough courage to say, "I hope you hit a homer!"

"Me too," said Chip with a smile. "Nice meetin' you too, Mr. Shannon..."

And with a tip of his cap, Chip strolled away in his easy country gait, returning to the steps of the dugout.

The game was tied 2–2 heading into the home half of the sixth. Waddell for St. Louis and Willett for the Tigers were pitching well for both sides and the fans had so far been treated to a defensive extravaganza, with sterling plays being turned all around the diamond.

The meat of the order was due up for Detroit with Ty Cobb set to lead off, but the crowd was witness to something rare – Cobb struck out on four pitches. Rube Waddell may have been aging and waning into the finality of his career, but he could still summon his speed when he needed to. It was just a year prior, 1908, when Waddell fanned 232 hitters. His personal career mark was a robust 349 strikeouts, set in 1904.

The next batter, Sam Crawford, managed a walk after fouling off successive pitches and working the count full. He checked his swing on ball four – a pitch that catcher Lou Criger unsuccessfully tried to steal with his attempts to frame the pitch, but the umpire did not fall for the ploy.

The next hitter was Chip Doolin and the crowd roared with approval as their rookie hero walked to the plate.

"C'mon, Chip!" urged a supportive Tyler Shannon, "Hit a good one!"

Chip smoothed the dirt over and surveyed the field before him. The fielders were playing him to pull, expecting Chip to hit it down the first base line. He gripped the bat, got set in the box and waited. Waddell got the sign, kicked and threw.

Chip stepped and swung at a knee-high fastball and ripped a furious shot down the third base line. St. Louis third bagger Hobe Ferris made a fine play when he dove and snagged it behind the bag, rushed to his feet and threw to first, but the umpire had already called it foul and Doolin was given another life.

The count went to three balls and one strike before Chip got hold of a curve ball and smacked it deep into the left field seats to give the Tigers a 4–2 lead. It was Chip's eighteenth round tripper of the season. The fans gave him a rousing applause as he crossed home plate for the fourth run. All of the Detroit hopeful knew that if Chip Doolin kept up the star-studded season he was enjoying, the Tigers would be going back to the World Series for certain.

By the top half of the seventh inning the sun had moved farther toward the horizon, signaling dusk, but it brought with it a drowning shadow that shrouded home plate, giving an even greater advantage to the pitcher.

Willett took the mound, now slated to a two-run lead, and St. Louis left fielder George Stone started the inning with a weak pop fly that second baseman Germany Schaefer handled with ease.

The next hitter was centerfielder Danny Hoffman, who was in the midst of his second season with the St. Louis club.

The first pitch to Hoffman was a ball. Then came, "Ball Two!" just missing the outside corner. Hoffman stepped out of the box. The count was in his favor and he'd be looking for the fastball from the Tiger hurler, and when he stepped back in, that's just what he got. Hoffman swung with all his might, but he was only able to pop it up into foul territory on the first base side. Doolin ran after the ball and before it started to come down from the sky, it had drifted toward the stands. Chip ran out of room and was now at the railing just before the front row seats, but he continued to track the ball. Just when it appeared the ball would be out of play, at the last second, Doolin dove into the stands, lunging for it. A sudden shriek was heard, and when the commotion settled, Chip's glove was off and he was seen tending to little Tyler Shannon, who was sitting awkwardly in his seat, his face covered with pain. Chip landed directly onto the youngster's leg – and let me tell you, the sound of that bone breaking was of the worst kind.

Those in attendance who were not aware of the special qualities that comprised Chipper Doolin, soon found out: They all watched the Tiger first baseman carefully and alertly pick the boy up and carry him through the stands and out to the gates, where he and Frank Shannon immediately hailed a cab to go to the hospital.

"Chip, really, he'll be fine. Go back – "

"No sir, Mr. Shannon. That ain't my way. I done it and I want to be sure it's fixed. I feel mighty awful."

Back in the ballpark, a fan held up Doolin's glove to a searching umpire – the ball was safely tucked inside the webbing and the batter was ruled *out*.

Claude Rossman took over for Doolin at first and the game resumed, but not before rustles and whispers and looks of exclamation and talk of admiration about the selfless act by Chip Doolin, echoed throughout the park; it rang through the hearts of every fan and it had the sports writers abuzz with headlines. I think that was when Chipper's legend

really began to grow, for after that day, his name transcended the game of baseball.

Meanwhile, Chip was at Tyler Shannon's bedside in the busy Detroit hospital.

"Mr. Doolin, all of the boys and girls in the ward next door would love it if you paid them a visit," said the doctor.

"Well, that's mighty kind to say and I reckon I'll bring myself to do it one day soon, but right now, I want to be sure my pal Tyler is okay."

"Oh, he'll be fine. It's a break, but it's not a bad one. He'll be back up and around in five to six weeks."

"Doc, I reckon any bone break is bad, and for this little guy to be outta commissions for that long… well, I'll tell ya what I'm gonna do, Tyler. I'm gonna get you a ball n' bat signed by the entire Detroit team and I'm gonna give you my here jersey shirt so you'll have your very own. Would you like that?"

"Oh, would I! Thanks, Mr. Doolin."

"And I'll be sure to get you some o' them seats for some other games."

"Alright! Daddy, we're gonna go to some more ball games and see Mr. Doolin! Mr. Doolin, will you hit a homer like you did today?"

"Well…" he said bashfully, "I'll try my best."

"Thank you once again, Chip," said a gracious Mr. Shannon, "you're a compliment to the game."

Chip's dignified feats earned him front page in the morning edition. Not only did he single-handedly ensure the care of his new, young friend, but he also had the game-winning home run in the Tigers eventual 4–3 win.

That next day, in a personally delivered package addressed to one "Tyler Shannon", was a ball and a bat signed by the entire Detroit team, and with them, Chip Doolin's Tiger jersey – number nine, signed by the famed rookie.

Yes, indeed...the legend and lore of Chip Doolin was only just beginning to grow.

Mama and Papas First Game

"My Mama and Papa don't know much about this here game I play, but I reckon they know plenty about playin' games. They might not even be able to recognize a baseball, but they sure do know the birthin' habits of a pig!"

-- Chip Doolin, Detroit Times, Spring 1909

Rain pelted the Detroit ballpark. Oversized puddles invaded the first base and third base playing areas and the thunder above, offered grim reminders of a possible rainout for the afternoon ball game.

I was in the Tiger dugout where I always sat before a game, before even a single fan walked through those gates – I really believe that there is no better place to collect one's thoughts and write a story than in a ballpark, sitting next to the field. There's a magical silence that I find inspirational and spiritual, staring out into the open, staring out onto a small portion of God's earth, specially manicured for a leather ball, a wooden bat, four bases and nine men. Maybe it was all those hits, dreams, diving stops and glory that infected me, or maybe it was all of the passion and science that filled every crevice of the game; the love for statistics and speculation, or maybe it was from when I was a boy, kneeling beside my bed and fervently praying to the Almighty to let my favorite team win. I was never quite sure then, nor am I now, but to me, baseball is a part of God, and so it *must* be a part of me too! It is a game that uses everything we've ever been given; every muscle, every tendon, every hope, and every ounce of soul; to many, the baseball field is a holy place where grown men pray before thousands without shame, and where Heaven's Angels seem to periodically roam, in the seeing-eye single, the bad hop and the wind-blown home run. I loved writing in an empty ballpark, and I still do...it's where I wrote this. But anyway...back to the story!

As the rain fell, the two groundskeepers peered out onto the field from the top step of the Detroit dugout. Streams of water, in fine lines, came down in front of them, but all they could do was wait and strategize how they might get the field ready and fit for a game of baseball, if they had to.

"What time is the first pitch today? Two or Three?"

"Three. But I reckon we might be able to push her to three-thirty if the rain stops."

"Yeah. We'll bring in some more dirt for them puddles."

"Yeah, we'll need that n' more."

Nap Lajoie and the Cleveland Naps had already arrived at the ballpark, only having to make the short trip from Chicago, where they had just wrapped up a three-game set with the White Sox.

While the rain showers doused the field, the team passed the time in the clubhouse, playing poker, sleeping and reading the morning newspaper.

Meanwhile, Chip and Eleanor were hosting Chip's parents, who were making their first visit to Detroit since their son had left home to try out for the Tigers. Believe it or not, they had never seen Chip play.

"Chipper, your Mama made you some o' your favorite stew – "

"It will give you some more muscle to knock some of them homers you hit, Chip," said his Mother.

"Thanks, Mama! I can use all the muscle I can get."

They were not sure how to react to Chip's roomy Detroit apartment. It had a cosmopolitan flair that infiltrated from the world around him. His parents gave special attention to the two paintings that decorated the walls.

"A painter named Claude Monet did that one, Mama – "

"Honey," interrupted Eleanor, "it's Mo-*nay*, not Mo-*net*."

"Yeah, Mama...Mo-Mo*nays*, like Elly says. A kind man and his wife brought it back for me from Paris. And that one there was done by an Eye-talian, but I can't say his name. I think it's beautiful – "

"Amedeo Modigliani," said Eleanor.

"I think it's nude! She ain't wearin' clothes, Chip!" exclaimed his father, his eyes widening.

"That's right and stop lookin' at her!" protested Chip's mother. "Chip, what are you doing with that in your home?"

"Oh, another couple we know invited us to their party," interjected Eleanor, "and they are such big fans of Chip, they took that right off their wall and gave it to him for keeping the Tigers in first place."

"Well, I ought to put them in their own place for having such a thing and corrupting my boy!"

"It's art, Mama."

"It's dirty, son!"

"By golly! She *is* a nude!" said his father.

"See? Who wants to look at her, besides your father? And he better – CUT IT OUT! Or no more whoopie for you, you dirty man – or apple pie!"

"Chip, you better call Mr. Jennings and see if there is a game today with this weather the way it is," said Eleanor, changing the subject.

Chip's parents were understandably a bit distraught over the sudden and drastic changes in their son's living habits, but Chip was coming into his own. He was becoming a man with opinions and theories and questions that were only his. He was defining his own character through new cultural exposures, vast educational experiences amongst society and through a select number of refined adults around him, who more often than not, were ardent fans of the Tigers. It all shaped his very innocent perception of the world. You have to realize…Chipper was a truly rare specimen. When he came to the big leagues he was like a calf whose knowledge of the world was limited to the size of his Virginia farm. He was now a long way from that farm in Somewhere, Virginia, and Eleanor had taken every step beside him. Although a bit more refined, she too was gaining and benefiting from the same experiences while doing her own part to establish herself in Detroit society, as the integral half of a talented baseball player who had fast become a celebrity – without Eleanor, I think a large part of Chip would have been empty. She was his fuel, and part of the secret power in his swing.

"The rain is stopping. The game starts at three-thirty."

"Will there be warm-ups?" asked Eleanor.

"Yes, darlin'. Two-fifteen."

THE ADVENTURES OF CHIP DOOLIN

⚾ ⚾ ⚾

When two o'clock came, streaks of sunshine could be seen in the far distance. The clouds were moving out.

"Okay boys. Take five swings each n' get out. Bush leads off," said manager Hughie Jennings. "We got Joss on the mound today, so you fellas best be ready."

Addie Joss overheard this from the sidelines where he was warming up. Wearing his Cleveland sweater, he turned toward Jennings only to offer an appreciative smile at the respect he was given. Thus far he had managed to achieve a stingy 1.36 earned run average. Only Ed Walsh of Chicago had a better one, but with low run support, Joss' record stood at just seven wins and four losses. (Unfortunately, it was just two years later when Joss would see both his career and his life end prematurely, in 1911 at age thirty-one, from a rare form of tubercular meningitis.) Nap Lajoie, Cleveland's player/manager, was the Indian's best hitter. His .331 average was forty-one points higher than the next best Cleveland hitter, centerfielder Joe Birmingham.

Chip's parents were given two of the best seats in the house, right next to the Detroit dugout. They sat with Eleanor and were given a complimentary bag of peanuts and a box of warm ribbon candy. They watched Chip take five whacks and send two balls over the left field fence during batting practice.

"That bat is a whole lot better than those broomsticks he used to use on the farm. After doin' his chores, he used to spend the afternoons hittin' those dang crab apples all over," reflected the elder Doolin.

"See? I think it's my stew that makes'em hit those balls like so – "

"I don't think he had a chance to taste your stew, Mama," said Mr. Doolin.

"Oh, you just shush! I helped raise the boy too, don't you think I know?"

"I was just sayin', Mama – "

"You don't just say nothin' of the sort. It was the stew I say – don't you think I know a little about this here game my son plays?"

"Well, he's my boy too, Mama, and I'm sorry I even opened up my mouth and – "

"As you always are!" said Mama Doolin, "And I've not forgotten about you lookin' at that nude woman, gettin' all excited as if she was some real life model!"

Three-thirty came quickly and the Detroit ballpark was suddenly filled with happy fans. Lajoie, Cy Young and Addie Joss posed for a picture for a young lad and Ty Cobb spent some moments signing autographs for some of the boys and girls huddled

THE ADVENTURES OF CHIP DOOLIN

around the dugout. Cobb, despite his derisive, hard-nosed reputation amongst the players of the game, never failed to give his attention to the youngsters.

Not long after, the players settled into their respective dugout, the umpire yelled, "Play ball!" and the game was underway.

⚾ ⚾ ⚾

Ed Summers retired the Cleveland team in order in the top of the first. In the bottom half, with one out, Indian third baseman Bill Bradley got the first chance to test the dirt around the third base bag, when Ty Cobb came up and hit a sharp grounder down the line; Bradley had to charge the ball when it started to die on the sopping grass. He got Cobb by only a step at first.

Joss, with dark brown hair cropping out from each side of his cap, then retired Crawford on a lazy fly to end the inning.

The crowd gave a thunderous applause to Chip Doolin when he came up to lead off the Tiger half of the second, in what was still a scoreless ballgame.

The first pitch from Joss was a beauty, a pitcher's pitch that caught the inside corner at the knees.

"Strike one!" said the umpire.

"Whatta you mean? You couldn't hit that one with a shovel!"

The next pitch came, just as high, but this time it caught the outside corner.

"Strike two!"

"You're crazy!" yelled the same voice from the stands, "You couldn't reach that one with a yard stick!"

Chip dug back in. Addie Adrian Joss got the sign. The pitch came.

"Steeerike three! Yer out!"

"*You* oughtta be out! That ball trimmed my boy's arm hair!"

Chip looked up. It was his father. He was now out of the stands and onto the field walking towards the umpire. The crowd's amusement created an audible stir throughout the park.

"Pop, what are you doin'?"

"I'm defendin' you! Those were lousy calls!"

"But you have to stay in your seat!"

"That guy needs his eyes checked!" said Pop Doolin. "He sees as much as a chicken with his head lopped off!"

"You! Yer outta here! Get out of this park!" screamed the ump at Chip's father.

"Oh, no sir. Please don't," pleaded Chip. "This is his first game. He never saw the likes of a real ball game."

"Oh, a first timer, eh?"

"That's right and you don't own this here park,"

said Chip's father, "so you can't throw me – "

"Oh, yes I can! You want to see me?"

"Papa! He can so n' you're embarrassin' me! Now you can't carry on like this."

"Mr. Doolin," said an approaching Hughie Jennings, "you're gonna get your son and his team in a whole mess o' trouble if you don't calm down."

"Mr. Umpire," said Chip, "can you give'em another chance?"

"Oh, I suppose so," he said with a grin, "but one more insult from you and you are out of this park for good!"

"But those weren't good balls, I say!"

"They were, Pop."

"Mr. Doolin," said Jennings, "the strike zone is from the armpits to the knees. And that guy pitchin' is one helluva pitcher. He put'em on the corners of the plate against your boy."

"He did? Well I sure couldn't hit no balls like them if I was swingin' my hog by his tail!"

"Well, Mr. Doolin, he *did* paint the corners with his pitches and I'm glad you chose to leave your hog at home," said the umpire.

Mr. Doolin peeked around the men to get a look at Joss, who kindly tipped his cap and gave a friendly smile.

"Now go on back, sit n' enjoy the game, Papa. The umpire said you can stay," said Chip.

"I can?"

"Yes, since you're a first-timer and all, and so long as you stop your yelling, you can stay," said the umpire.

Mr. Doolin removed his hat to scratch his head.

"C'mon Papa, I'll walk you back."

Chip walked his father back to the stands amidst chuckles by the surrounding news reporters, and I must admit that I got a real good laugh out of it too.

"Chipper, I warned your father to be quiet."

"Thanks, Mama. It's okay."

"I thought my stew gave you muscle?"

"Oh, it does Mama. I'll get'em next time."

Before Chip went back to the dugout, he stopped to have a word with the reporters. "Hey, fellas. Please don't laugh at someone cuz they don't know. It's just not nice to make fun o' people who don't know no better. This here game ain't his experience. But he sure raised me awlright and I'm glad he's my Papa."

"We're sorry, Chip."

"Yeah, awfully sorry Chipper. Won't happen again."

"Thanks, fellas," said Chip.

The score remained 0-0 as they went into the last of the ninth. Joss had stifled the Tiger batsmen, yielding just two hits so far, one by Donie Bush in the fourth and another by Matty McIntyre in the sixth.

With two out in the home half of the ninth, Ty Cobb and Sam Crawford banged consecutive singles, line drive hits that were driven into left-centerfield.

The next batter was Chipper, with yet another chance to lift the Tigers to a dramatic win. He always seemed to have a knack for being in a spot where he could become a hero, and I don't recall too many times when he failed to deliver.

I remember Joss had already retired Chip three times that day, giving him the advantage. As sweat dripped from his brow Chip stepped in and waited for the pitch. The imposing Joss stared in from atop the mound, ready to bear down and fire another one. He wound, kicked and threw.

"Strike one!"

It was that same pitch, on the inside corner at the knees that he had been getting him out on all day. Chip adjusted his stance, opening it up just a bit. He lowered his hands on the bat as far as he could, until they were snug against the knob. He dug his back foot in, and waited once more. The next pitch was on the outside corner at the knees. Chip swung the bat toward left field and connected! He hit a soft, opposite-field liner that was sinking fast!

Wilbur Good gave chase from left field. The ball was headed toward the foul line. Good ran as hard as he could and at the last possible second, he went into an outstretched dive to try and save the game, while Cobb raced around third and headed for home! Good landed and tumbled end over end! The umpire ran out to see whether he had the ball. When Good got up off the ground, that beautiful, dirty, muddied ball, with its muddied strings, was lying under him, resting on the wet, glistening grass, its faded leather shine barely visible in the damp night air, the product of another Tiger win.

"It was that stew, Mama! It was that stew!" Chip later exclaimed, hugging his mother.

"See! He *did* have some!" said Mama Doolin, nudging her husband.

"That's my boy, Chipper," said his father, with tears welling in his eyes. "We're real proud o' you."

"Oh, boy. There he goes, Chipper. Your father's gonna get all sentimental and blow his nose twenty times...try and make me forget he was lookin' at that nude woman in your paintin'..."

"Well, Mama...would you rather have'em look at one that was alive n' real?"

"Sure...he could look at me," said Mama Doolin, grabbing her husband's hand to hold.

Going Back to School

It was an off day for the Tiger ball club before they were to start a four-game series against the rival Philadelphia Athletics. The Athletics had won six straight games and threatened Chip's Detroit club at the top of the standings. It was going to be a tough and competitive series, and the fans in the city of Detroit expected as much, wildly anticipating a fierce clash of talent. Tickets for the four games were already sold out, accounting for all of the 8500 chairs in Bennett Park, not including the 'unofficial' bodies that would crowd the foul lines in left and right field; the press boys around the dugouts; the folks standing in the grandstand area who managed to 'sneak' in for a small fee paid to the ushers, and of course, those distinguished enough to be allowed to sit in lawn chairs just beyond the front row seats. In all, Detroit management was expecting roughly 14000 fans for each game of the series.

Rumors circulated that there might be a few

tickets left over, but most of those would be given away in newspaper contests or raffles. It was a heated mid-summer meeting between two teams vying for the playoffs, and pennant fever had gripped Detroit, Michigan, all the way up through the Great Lakes. It was a great time to be a baseball fan.

Men in barber shops, friends in smoking parlors, women at civic meetings and tea parties, and pals playing cards, debated, discussed or preached who the better team was. Who was the more talented pair, Baker and Collins? Or Cobb and Crawford? Who was the best first bagger, Chip Doolin or Harry Davis? Could Detroit's Mullin and Willet beat Philly's star tandem of Eddie Plank and Chief Bender?

The fervor that came with the series weighed heavily over the city, and no one felt it more than the players themselves, especially a first year player who had suddenly become a star, like Chip Doolin.

Chip and Eleanor strolled arm in arm along the tree-lined street, taking advantage of the off-day on the baseball schedule, before the start of the series. It was a dandy day to get out, temperate and sunny, summer as it should be. Summer's sounds abounded – bird chirps and the buzzing bees, ice cream stands and crowded soda fountains, and the folly of children playing games, swimming or sitting on the porch with their Mom and Dad eating homemade cherry pie. The flowers were in such bloom one could almost hear their colors: whispery reds, humming blues, startling whites, impassioned purple, just as one could attach the sounds of spoken pleasantries to the smiles of neighbors and people in the neighborhood who smiled voluminous, sunny smiles; smiled because they felt that way from the sun or because trouble of any kind seemed worlds away on this perfect day. It was the decade of life and the way things were.

"This is nice..." said Eleanor, "nice to spend a whole day with you."

"Sure is. I like havin' my arm in yours," said Chip. "Say, would you like to stop n' get a soda pop, Elly? I think they're givin' away free carnations to all the ladies."

"I know you would like one, so yes, let's stop. Then we'll walk to the school and turn back."

"Are ya feelin' awlright, Elly?"

"Oh, just a little stomach ache is all."

Later, as they walked past a schoolhouse – the same schoolhouse that I attended as a child – an older gentleman came running out through its doors, "Chip Doolin! Chip Doolin! Why, aren't you the great Chipper Doolin of the mighty *Detroit Tigers*?"

"I reckon I am, sir," said Chip, holding out his

hand to greet the fast approaching man. "Mighty fine to have the pleasure of meeting you – "

"Oh, no, no! The pleasure is mine! What an honor to meet a model to all boys and girls."

"Why, thank you. Are you the teacher of this here board house?" said Chip.

"Honey," interrupted Eleanor, "it is a schoolhouse. I don't think the children *live* here."

"I apologize Mister, but my vocab-lary just ain't the best. In fact, I'm tryin' to improve on it – "

"No apology necessary. That is correct, Mrs. Doolin. We have four teachers in our school, and I am one of them," said the man, "but I am also the Schoolmaster, and the children here would be tickled to death if you could spare just a few moments and give them a surprise visit – and maybe say a few words!"

"Oh, Chip, go ahead in – "

"You sure, Elly? Cuz I promised you no baseball stuff on my off day?"

"But this is for the children," said Eleanor. "This isn't baseball stuff. The joy they'll have in their eyes just seeing you – "

"I'd be mighty glad, sir, to oblige your request," said Chip.

"Great!" said the tall, lanky Schoolmaster, and as they were walking into the school, he said with excitement, "You know, I used to play baseball some years back...Bill Stellberger is my name, and after sandlot ball, I played one professional game for the Providence Grays, the year after they won the championship.

"What a real swell treat that was," continued Stellberger. "I pitched in one game – start to finish – I did not strike out anybody, failed to get a hit myself, and we lost, but what a joy and an honor to have played just that one game. That was when most of us still did not wear ball gloves, except for maybe the catcher and the first bagger, and only if they felt like it."

⚾ ⚾ ⚾

All of the boys and girls in the school were told to quickly gather themselves, tuck in their shirts, flatten their dresses and check their hair, because they were about to be surprised by "a very important guest. A very important guest indeed! Important to all of you, and to every breathing baseball fan in Detroit!" said Mr. Stellberger.

Boys wearing knickers and girls wearing dresses emptied from all four classrooms and politely assembled into the lecture hall.

On Mr. Stellberger's signal, Chip and Eleanor Doolin emerged from around a corner, hand in hand, and entered the hall. There was something in that room that day that changed Chip Doolin for the rest of his life. I could never figure out what it was and neither could he. In later years, every time I asked Chip, his only reply was, "I just can't explain it," and it wasn't because of his lack of words, because as an older man, after his ball playing days, Chip became a very astute and eloquent speaker.

Anyway, back at that schoolhouse, the children erupted into a booming and thunderous roar at the sight of their big league idol. Chip was visibly moved by the reception. All of the youthful energy, all of the wiry young souls seated politely like grown adults in miniature bodies, with wide eyes looking from Chip to the reaction of their friends and classmates, measuring whether it was the same level of astonishment as their own. Children with slightly turned up mouths and button noses and candy gum curls and buoyancy in their reddened cheeks! Chip was taken up in all of it, and when Eleanor turned to her husband, the man she had known since her own youth, she saw tears in his eyes, which made hers fill up too. Chip had a glow about him; something to do with the enamorment he felt for the children and the energy in the room.

When the cheers subsided, Chip remained in awe – in revelation...he was in the midst of his own epiphany.

"I..." he stumbled, "golly, it's such a mighty fine

honor to be here. Thank you for receiving me in such a way. A man is certainly blessed when he has such...such wonderful n' beautiful boys n' girls givin'em their support n' applause like so – "

A boy in the front row raised his hand. Chip pointed to him and softly said, "What can I do for ya, little buddy?"

"Mr...Mr. Doolin, can you hit a homer for all of us tomorrow?"

Another gleeful roar came from the children, "Yeah! Yeah! Could you? Could you please?" they screamed.

"Well, boys n' girls, that Ath-letic club is a mighty tough club, but just for you all, I'm gonna try extra hard to hit one."

"Well students," interrupted Mr. Stellberger, "we cannot keep Mr. Doolin, after all, this was a surprise visit for him too – "

The sounds of dejection traveled through the lunchroom. Chip looked at Eleanor. She grabbed his arm with both hands and held it tight.

"Mr. Stellberger, sir?"

"Yes, Chip?"

"Before they're excused for their summer break, I'd be mighty pleased to stay a while longer n' sign some autographs if they like."

I don't need to tell you how *that* suggestion went over with the children. Chipper stayed until he gave each and every one of those children an autograph.

Just before Chip and Eleanor left the school that day, Mr. Stellberger had one more request. "Say, you wouldn't happen to have any extra tickets for the series, would you? They are so difficult to come by."

"As a matter of fact I do," said Chip, reaching into his shirt pocket and pulling out two tickets. "My Mom n' Pop were supposed to go but Pop's hip's been botherin'em on accounts of that Virginian humidity. You see it gets real damp down there on the farm n' with all the work to be done, they regretted to mention they won't be comin' to the opener tomorrow."

"Oh, my! Front row! Thanks Mr. Doolin, I really appreciate this!"

"We appreciate you asking us into your school. The children are so well behaved and absolutely adorable," said Eleanor.

"Come anytime! Knock'em dead tomorrow, Chipper. Watch out for Plank's curve ball. He's got a good one."

The electric spirit of baseball descended on the park. There was the hot smell of roasted peanuts and candy in the air. The summer season donned the bleachers and decorated the people, who arrived in summer hats and summer suits. Players from both teams were warming up along the foul lines – baseballs smacking against leather. The players were practically sharing space with the fans, who were also on the field. Don't forget, this was 1909 and fans were *allowed* past the seats, and it was quite a sight to see, as they cascaded down from the packed stands like a waterfall.

When the game began, the electricity only intensified. It was such a fierce rivalry that fights broke out amongst rival fans. It was not unusual to see blood-spattered shirts.

After Mullin retired Collins, Murphy and Home run Baker in the top of the first, the Tiger front three of Donie Bush, Ty Cobb and Chip Doolin were ready to face Philly's ace pitcher and the always intimidating, Eddie Plank.

On a 2-2 count, Bush struck out on a big, oval curve that had him lunging far ahead of it.

Ty Cobb hit a 'comebacker' to the mound, Plank fielded it cleanly and threw him out. On his way back to the dugout, Cobb had some words for Plank, "I'll get you next time," he said with a snare, before taking a seat on the bench.

Then, up to the plate stepped the lefty, Chip Doolin, and the crowd went wild. (Manager Jennings had moved Chip to the clean-up spot on account of his power, but for this series, Jennings wanted him back up in the three slot of the order.) He dug his back foot into the rich dirt until his spikes were securely planted. He cocked his bat at the ready and remembered all those effervescent, young faces at Mr. Stellberger's wonderful schoolhouse. All of those children, just the way they set their eyes on him, looking up with such reverie and wonder, made Chip grasp the bat in an extra special way. When I saw him move his hands back even more, to generate as much power as he could, I knew Chip was ready to swing for the fences, an extra special swing for all of those extra special children who were now extra special memories in his heart.

Well...you want to know what happened next? What if I told you that Chip extinguished all of the hopes of Athletic fans everywhere, in his very first at bat? Because that's just what he did.

Edward Stewart Plank's very first pitch to Chipper Doolin was a curve ball, and when it came, it went, straight over the right field fence on a perfect and gorgeous line, like a rocket that sailed into yonder. It had to have been one of the smoothest swings the baseball gods had ever seen.

The game ended in another Tiger victory, 4-1. The fourth run scored on a Doolin single in the eighth inning. The Tigers went on to split the series with the Athletics, but in the process they staved off the Philadelphia club, preventing them from gaining ground, and the Tigers first place standing remained.

Later that evening, as Eleanor and Chip were getting ready for bed, Eleanor said, "I think I would like to go back to school one day and further my education."

"If you desires to betters yourself," said Chip, "that's entirely okay with me. What's best for you is the same for us. Whatever you decide is best – a child of our own first or you makin' yourself more smart so you can do more in this world. I know I can't play ball forever – "

"I love you, Chip Doolin."

"Aww, I love you too, Elly. That was a fine game today wasn't it?"

"You made them all so happy."

"Yeah, I hope I did."

Yes, Boys...That's my Sister

The day she learned that her husband had just been offered a job with a prestigious New York City law firm, Norma Doolin got so excited she could not refrain herself from jumping up and down in the couple's three-room flat.

She jumped and jumped, arms flailing, cheeks smiling, pregnant belly bobbing, and her eyes – oh, those eyes. They were said to be the biggest blue eyes in all of Virginia!

"Those eyes...why those eyes could stop a train, a racing horse and an army of charging soldiers!" proclaimed the town Sheriff when Norma was still a girl. "When she becomes a woman she'll be a real looker for sure."

Indeed she was, for at the age of eighteen, when she boarded her very first train en route to New York, with plans to become an actress fresh on her mind, she met her future husband who was in the row across from her. He was a man who could not stand the sight of a young lady in distress, a woman like Norma, crying hysterically and already homesick before the train left the platform; big tears streaming down her saddened cheeks as she waved goodbye to her parents through the window. When Arthur reached across with his handkerchief to comfort and to dab one of the big, oval tears, he suddenly, unexpectedly beheld those eyes. That was it. Arthur was hooked. They were married not six months after.

Returning back to that day of excitement in the flat: Norma's excitement grew to such a pitch and a frenzy that she induced herself into labor, and that was how, doctors reasoned, the baby came out already possessed with hyperactivity...and a set of eyes that rivaled his mother's.

Chip and Norma would exchange short letters or rather, short quips throughout the years, but they never had a chance to grow terribly close, mainly because Chip was just seven years old when Norma left home in search of bigger adventures, and then there was the great distance in travel that separated them.

Dear Norma,

Hi, this is yur brother Chipper. Just wanted to say hello and I hope you ain't sick or nothin'. I hit another homer. The fans seem to like me when I hitem and I like them too. Say hello to Arthur an to yur sun, I always forgit his name even though he's my blood. Sorry Norma. I love you.

    Yur brother,
    Chip

Or,

Dear Norma,

Hello, this is Chip agan. I'll be in NY nex month to play the Hilanders. Wanna come watch? Say hello to Arthur and yur sun William.

    Love, Chip

Dear Chip,

It was nice to hear from you and to receive your letter. Your nephew's name is not William, it is Walter. Arthur said you hit against someone with the same name, "Walter Johnson"? Anyway, perhaps I can see you, but awful busy are my days, caring for Walter, cooking for Arthur, decorating the home, etc. I will put it on my calendar, but I think I might have a tea party planned with the other lawyer's wives. Well, little brother, I have to go. Arthur said to keep hitting those homers.

Love,
Norma

P.S. I keep telling you, there is not such a word as "wanna". It is as much of a word as "ain't", which as I have told you, is <u>not</u> a word. Daddy was a bad influence in the way of speaking habits, as was where we were raised. Wanna = <u>want to</u>, just as ain't = <u>is not</u> or <u>am not</u>. Also, "agan" is spelled "again", and "yur" is spelled "your". So

THE ADVENTURES OF CHIP DOOLIN

many other corrections to make, but I've run out of paper!

When Chip's Detroit club visited New York for the second time during his rookie season, he arrived to a tragedy. Norma's husband, Arthur, was struck and killed the day before by a speeding horse-drawn carriage as he crossed the street with his head down, reading the newspaper – he had it opened to the sports page. At the time of the accident, Policemen were chasing the man driving the carriage. Arthur was apparently knocked to the ground unconscious and died later in the evening from head wounds, with Norma and little Walter by his side.

At first, Chip was speechless. He had never been formally introduced to such tragedy. He had never been terribly close to anyone who had passed on. He did not know his grandparents on his mother's side because death took them both within six months – before Chip was yet two – tuberculosis being the fatal nemesis, and his grandparents on his father's side were still amongst the living, but lived afar, in Cork City, Ireland. Suffice to say, Chip was beside himself.

"Norma...gee, Norma," was all Chip could say, while missing three games in the four-game New York series to tend to his sister and go to funeral services. He went hitless with three strikeouts in the series finale.

"Norma..." said Chip, before his team boarded the train to go back to Detroit, "why don't you n' lil' Walter come back with us n' stay with Elly n' me – at least for a little while – aww, Norma I'm awfully sorry..." and Chip burst into tears over the sight of his depressed sister. She was immersed in her own agony of sudden loss, faced with raising a boy on her own, and therefore realizing she hadn't the allowance of extended sorrow or mourning.

"I don't know what to do, Chipper," said a tearful Norma, with large tears from her big, blue eyes falling and drenching the carpet. For the first time since Chip was a boy, they hugged in comfort.

"Chip, remember when you were little, and you ran out of the barn crying because you got bitten by a spider?"

"Yes, I sure do. You hugged me n' made it feel all better – you took care o' me. Now let me take care o' you n' lil' Walter."

"Yeah?"

"Yeah. It's best. And plus, you can teach me all them words I ain't supposed to say, that ain't words," said Chip, with a wink and a smile.

Within an hour, Norma's New York apartment was locked and shut; her New York dreams meeting an unfortunate and similar fate. The home she had made with Arthur, with all of his accents and possessions still adorning the premises – his shirt draped across the rocking chair, his favorite coffee mug on the table still half-filled with expired coffee, and his wool hat with the silk band hanging lifeless on a hook, as if begging to cover a familiar head – was closed behind her. She slid the key into the keyhole one final time and walked away.

With Chip carrying three bags of luggage and Norma carrying Walter, they boarded the Tiger team train.

⚾ ⚾ ⚾

As the train rolled toward Michigan, Norma had a chance to get acquainted with her brother's Tiger teammates and manager.

"On behalf of the whole Detroit club, please accept our heartfelt condolences. We are all truly sorry for your sudden loss," said Hughie Jennings.

"Thank you," said Norma.

When Chip introduced his teammates and friends to his sister, they all walked away whispering to themselves, seeing double and bumping into each other.

"Did you see those eyes?"

"A man could get lost in there! And be happy at the same time!"

"She's sure a fine lady and one to die for."

"I feel bad for her husband, the poor guy. Now

he has to watch from Heaven as every single man on earth tries to make that gorgeous dame his wife."

"Well, if I had those eyes to look into every morning, I'd never leave the house."

"Hey, Chipper," said Matty McIntyre, pulling Chip aside, "do you think…do you think that…"

"What is it, Matty?"

"Well, I know it's all so soon n' all, and I don't mean no disrespect, Chipper, honest I don't – "

"Doggone it, Matty Mac, spit it out!" said Chip.

"It's your sister, Chip. She's so – so beautiful, and I was wonderin' if we all might be able to go to a picture show together, or somethin'."

"Gee, Matty. Maybe as acquaint-ces, but she is not lookin' to get all tangled up right fast – "

"I know. I know – "

"This here is a tragedee, and I ain't – I mean…I am not so sure how she'll receive a ballplayer. She was married to a real intellekchull."

"I know how to read, Chip, if that's what you be askin' – "

"I know you can read, Matty – aww, look pal, I'll see what I can do. It will be good for her to keep active n' her mind offuh things – "

"Thanks, Chipper. You're a pal – "

"Hey, Matty," said Chip, grabbing his shoulder, "you just don't go n' lose yourself n' forget she's my sister."

THE ADVENTURES OF CHIP DOOLIN

⚾ ⚾ ⚾

When Boston came into Detroit for a four game set, the Detroit press got its first look at the Tiger's newest spectator and fan, and was she a dandy!

"Yes, boys, that there is my sister. Be sure to write kind things about'er, eh boys?"

"Sure thing, Chipper."

"Hey Chip, if my eyes miss your at-bats or any part of the game, it will be on account of them getting glued some place else," said one of the reporters.

"What's her name, Chipper?" asked another reporter.

"Her name is Norma, boys," said Chip, while standing near the on-deck circle.

Norma was within earshot of the discussions, and was obviously flattered by the attention, because her cheeks suddenly took on the hue of a pair of red delicious apples. She had joined Eleanor in the front row with little Walter on her lap.

"Hey, Norma!" said a reporter. "Do you like the game of baseball?"

Norma was hesitant to answer, unaccustomed to being the center of public attention.

"Now, boys," said Chip, "let her alone so she can – "

"Why I think it is a grand game and good for every young boy," said Norma with a display of charm, and after she finished she looked Chip right in the eyes with a smile fit for a screen star.

"That's a quote to use," said one reporter, scribbling in his pad.

"Yep, definitely," echoed another.

"Sure is! Especially from a lady that looks like that."

Matty McIntyre, the Tiger leftfielder, was watching the sideshow with interest from the top step of the dugout. He figured he had better make a move, lest any notoriety get between him and the opportunity to date one of Detroit's newest and finest spectacles.

"Pardon me, ma'am," said Matty, with his ball cap over his heart, "I don't believe we have met, and to save you from these here *ravenous* press boys, I wanted to *formally* introduce myself. My name is Matty McIntyre and I missed the honor of meetin' you on the train."

The reporters suddenly went into hush mode so they could hear every word...oh, c'mon! To be a good reporter or writer you *have* to eavesdrop...

"I play left field," he said, coyly lowering his head.

"Hello Matty," said Norma, "It is a pleasure to meet you as well."

"This is a real swell pal o'mine," said Chip, approaching the seats. "Hey Matty, we was all gonna go to a show later this week – "

"We *were* going...Chipper," said Norma, with apprehension in her eyes.

"Oh...uh, we *were* all going to be going – "

"Yes, we'll have to see," said Norma, "I am not sure how I will be feeling and if Walter – "

"Oh, Norma, if I may – " said Matty, "if my going *prohibits* you from going, then I won't go."

"Oh, well it isn't that – " started Norma.

"But I'd be much obliged and the most honored and privileged man in all of Detroit if you did go – why I'd be tickled with joy!"

"Tickled? Did he just say, 'tickled'?" whispered a reporter friend of mine.

Yes, I was one of those reporters listening in on this conversation that day, and Matty McIntyre really *did* use the word "tickled". In fact, he must have brought his whole toolbox of words over to Norma's seat, because I swear he was using words that were complete strangers to his mouth – not that "tickled" is a big word, but for Matty, and in the context he was using it, he might as well have been giving a course lecture on the anatomy of the English language.

However, it must have worked because there actually seemed to be a moment of silence in the midst of that noisy ballpark, when Norma looked and saw nothing but kindness in Matty McIntyre's soft and boyish brown eyes. "Well..." said Norma, "those are very kind words, thank you. And all right, I will go. It is rather hard for me right now and will be for some time. I hope you – "

"I understand...and – and well, I – I have to go now. I have to get ready for the game. Mighty fine meeting you," said Matty. He stuck his hand out and received her hand the way a gentleman should, careful not to squeeze too tight, but applying just the right firmness.

"Bye, now," he said, walking backwards with the hesitancy of a boy filled with lust and awe, "B – Bye..."

Norma could only nod and giggle at the unabashed display of affection.

⚾ ⚾ ⚾

Feeling gleeful and celebratory, Matty McIntyre got four hits that day, and made a spectacular catch in the outfield, to pace Detroit's 5-3 win over Boston. Chip added a two-run double that missed being a home run by just a few feet.

"Hey, Matty," Chip said after the game, "Where'd you get all them long words you was sayin'? "Ravnous" n' such?"

"Well, Chipper...don't tell her, but I did me some real readin' last night, and I learned some words I could use."

"Oh, that's just swell, Matty – this whole thing makin' you read n' all. What was the name o' the book?"

"*The Dictionary,*" said Matty with a proud smile.

Close Call, Chipper *or* Welcome to the Windy City

The 1909 Chicago White Sox were a feisty ball club. They always put up a fight. If they had a better hitter or two they would have been at the top of the division, since scoring enough runs was their biggest problem; their Achilles heel, always snake-bit by just one or two runs. They were ten games behind Detroit in the standings, and struggling to stay ahead of New York for fourth place in the division. The White Sox had a strong pitching staff that kept them close, and midway through the season Frank Smith and Ed Walsh were the main anchors, with Jim Scott and Doc White – when healthy – handling the brunt of the work load. The winds were swirling something fierce when the first place Tigers came in to play four games, which included a Saturday doubleheader.

"How do you feel today?" said Ty Cobb to Ed Summers, who was warming up along the foul line.

THE ADVENTURES OF CHIP DOOLIN

"Well, with this wind, I better try and keep my pitches low. If I don't, even this club will knock the ball around this park like it's a Mexican jumpin' bean! Other than that, Ty, I feel awlright," said Summers.

"Is it usually this windy up here in July?" asked Chip.

"Well, pal," said Ty, "this is a bit uncommon, cuz it's extra bad up here today – " and suddenly, a wicked gust came and blew his hat clear off his head. "I reckon they'll be plenty of wind-blown doubles today!" said Cobb, as he went to chase his cap that continued to travel out to the right field fence.

"There's a bird in that hat!" said Charley O'Leary, who had to raise his voice to compete with the sound of the wind.

The winds howled like a team of trumpets through Southside Park, sending debris – hats, newspapers, candy wrappers, peanut bags and peanut shells – asunder. There was an odd flavor in the currents, in the very way they whipped about, as if holding some austere message delivered from nature; like some fate being carried and unfurled throughout the ballpark. I remember it was downright spooky, as though there was a whole family of ghosts flying around. One of the groundskeepers even thought he saw an odd figure – like a shadowy specter – walking around in left field, giving the day and the elements an added mystery.

"This wind is strong enough to even throw a dog," said Boss Schmidt, grabbing a seat in the dugout.

"What kind of dog?" asked Sam Crawford.

"A terrier."

"Nah. At least a beagle. This stuff's bad. It'll be an adventure out there for sure today. Heck, even the press boys are under cover.

You bet we were!

Frank Smith, who was leading the league in strikeouts and complete games took the mound for the ChiSox, with his hat pulled as low as it would go on his head. The first Tiger batter he faced was Donie Bush.

"Geez..." said Donie to the umpire, Billy Evans, "the ball's gonna blow back to the pitcher before it reaches home plate!"

"Then maybe you better swing so it looks like you hit it," said the Chicago catcher *and* manager, Billy Sullivan.

"Yes, I suppose I better, Sully, because your eyes are tearing so bad from this here wind, you'll need water goggles to see the ball before it hits you smack in the jaw."

"If you don't step in the box, I'm gonna bust your

jaw!" said Sully with a smile.

On the very first pitch, Bush hit a high pop-up that started on the shortstop side of the diamond, but ended out of play on the first base side.

"Hey Sully..." said umpire Evans, who was also a preacher, "did your team do something to offend the Lord?"

"Not that I know of."

"Well, this is the most wicked wind I ever did see in a ballpark, and I guess someone upstairs just did not want your shortstop to catch that ball."

"Well, Mr. Umpire, maybe you're right, and maybe someone upstairs just wanted that boy in the fourth row to have that ball as a souvenir," said Sullivan

Donie Bush hit a weak grounder to the mound that Smith handled with ease.

The next batter, Ty Cobb, hit a first pitch liner to left that looked like it might go for at least a triple, but the wind worked against Cobb and slowed it down enough for Patsy Dougherty to make the putout.

Next up was Doolin, and the Chicago crowd gave him a warm welcome. Like every other baseball fan on earth, they were well aware of his seasonal heroics.

"These sure are brave souls in these stands. Darn brave to bear these crazy elements, if ya ask me," said Chip.

"Well now, rookie," said Sullivan, "nobody asked ya, but there's your difference between Chicago and Detroit. But they sure seem to like you here. If ever you get tired of them Tigers, I'd take you in less than a heartbeat. We can use a bat like yours."

"Lord knows that!" said umpire Evans.

The first pitch from Smith was so close to Chip's chin that he had to duck away at the last second, sending his hat flying off his head, it then got caught in a swirl of wind that carried it into the crowd.

"Now do you think the Lord is mad at him too?" asked Sullivan.

"Don't get smart, Sully. Just maybe *that* boy is *supposed* to have that cap," said a smirking Evans.

"But I don't have another that fits my head," said Chip.

"Darn, Doolin, is your head that big that there ain't no other hat?" said Sullivan.

"Hey, what's the problem?" yelled Jennings from the bench.

"Now your boy hasn't a ball cap," said Evans.

"Rossman," said Jennings, "go out there n' give Chip your cap."

"But it won't fit'em."

"Well, cut it on the side – "

"Cut my ball cap?"

"That's what I said – "

"But with what?"

"With what? Your fingers! Geez, Rossman, was your Mama n' Papa scarecrows? Or maybe that was you they caught sniffin' round the brain factory – get the scissors outta the doctor kit there. And hurry!"

By this time Chipper had walked back to the bench.

"Sorry, Chip. We got a boy here thinks he can cut wool with his fingers."

"Well, I'm mighty appreciative that Claude's givin' up his cap for me."

"He insisted on it, Chipper. The same way he gave up his first base job to you."

Chip cracked an awkward smile and walked back to the batter's box.

"You all set now, rookie?"

"Sure am, Mr. Sullivan."

"Okay, I'll tell Smitty not to throw you anymore chin music or we might go through every cap in the house."

The very next pitch Chip hit on the button and sent it high and deep toward centerfield. As the centerfielder started back, the wicked winds stirred again and got hold of the ball, sending it on a bend toward right, which now had both outfielders in pursuit – Altizer and Hahn. It seemed the national jet stream suddenly moved and dropped into the Chicago outfield. The outfielders chased and chased, while the wind dallied and played with the leather ball. When it finally started its fall from the sky, Altizer and Hahn were side-by-side flailing left and right like a comedy duo, trying to stay under it. In the meantime, Chip was rounding second base and was on his way to third. At the last second, the winds jerked the ball again and it hit off the right field fence. Both outfielders quickly tried to pick the ball up to throw it in, but they collided. The ball came to a rest between them, as if part of some cruel joke; Altizer and Hahn, dumbfounded by the turn of events, could do nothing but look at each other. Much of the capacity crowd was confused, unsure of whether to roar in laughter or stare in perplexity and amazement. Chip crossed home plate for an inside-the-park home run. To this day it was one of the most bizarre episodes I have ever seen occur on a ball field, but like I said, there was something crazy in those winds that day.

Things took a turn for the worse in the home half of the sixth. Freddy Parent, the Chicago shortstop, was at the plate. The count was no balls and two strikes. The Tigers had the lead, 4-3, but all seven runs were the result of Mother Nature – *she* had seven RBI's on the day, her great winds playing a role in every one.

Parent was expecting a two-strike fastball from Ed Summers, but instead he got a curveball. Parent was caught off-balance and in a defensive swing, hit a pop fly on the first base side. That's when they came again. Yes, those damn winds! They came roaring through once more.

"Oh, no...not again," said a frustrated manager Jennings, removing his hat and waiting for the outcome, as Doolin gave chase to the pop-up.

Chip pursued the ball from fair territory into foul territory, closer and closer to the stands.

Right fielder Sam Crawford tried to yell to Chip that he was fast running out of room, but because of the wind, Chip never heard him or his catcher Stanage, who gave the same warning, "Chip, look out!"

He somehow forgot himself. Or maybe it was the entrancement of the wind or the entrapment of Mother Nature...all at once he picked up speed, and running at full tilt, Chip followed the ball into the stands with a CRASH!

He lay motionless, sprawled out atop a pair of second row seats, with a stream of blood running down the side of his head. The events that followed are somewhat of a blur to me because they happened so fast. I can remember them in pieces. I do recall that utter commotion seized the ballpark.

"I am calling this game right now on account of

that wind. It is simply too darn dangerous and too strong for a baseball," Umpire Evans said to Chicago skipper, Billy Sullivan, before heralding throughout the park, "This game is called! The game is over! Due to hazardous weather conditions, the game is called!"

I heard someone yell, "Get a doctor! Is there a doctor in the house?" The voice sounded familiar and I wanted to know who owned it. I looked up to see famed Chicago news reporter, Ring Lardner, who had been sitting behind the Tiger dugout, hoping to complete a feature story he had started on Chip.

When Lardner's voice rang out, the entire ballpark was silenced. Not a single fan left the park, every one of them fastened to their seat, hoping for some sign of movement from the star first bagger. I must admit we were all pretty scared for Chipper. I had a hollow pang in my gut that signaled something was seriously wrong.

When Chip's first base mitt was removed with caution from his hand, the ball was nestled inside – but it went without mention. No one cared about baseball at that moment. Instead, the sanctity of life of a fine young man and model citizen was on the minds of every person in the ballpark; and the sobering mood infected the day, painting a somber expression on the face of every fan.

THE ADVENTURES OF CHIP DOOLIN

Chip was carefully removed on a stretcher and rushed to the local hospital, still unconscious. The fans followed the horse-drawn ambulance, and crowded outside the hospital entrance.

"Someone wire Eleanor. Get'er here immediately – "

"I'll do that," said Matty McIntyre, "I'll dial his sister, Norma."

⚾ ⚾ ⚾

The hours passed; eight of them to be exact. It was well past dinnertime when Chip finally awoke.

"Elly…" said Chip, "hello, darlin'."

"Hi, sweetheart," she said, with worry on her face.

"What's wrong? Mr. Jennings – Norma, Matty… why doggone it, why are ya'll here lookin' at me funny? Where am I –"

"Hello, Chip. My name is Dr. Landis. You bumped your head pretty good, and you are in a hospital here in Chicago, under my care."

"I got a head bump that landed me in the hospital? Why don't I remember it happenin'? And what's the drognosis?"

"Do you want the *prognosis* or the *diagnosis*?" asked the doctor.

Chip cocked his head in a curious way at Dr.

Landis, not fully comprehending either word, but in the midst of his befuddlement there was a positive sign – his vitality was winding up again.

"All ya'll came here from Detroit to see me?"

"Chip, honey," said Eleanor, "You were knocked unconscious and it looked very serious."

"I don't understand."

"What's not to understand?" said Jennings.

"If I was unconscious, where'd my conscious go?"

"Eh...*conscience* you mean to say, Chipper," said Jennings. "And yours went n' slipped under the second row seats is where your conscience gone."

"You are going to be just fine, Chip, but my recommendation is to keep you out of the lineup for a day or two," said the doctor.

"Hold on here!" said Chip, rising in his bed and for the first time noticing his new hospital attire. "And who went n' changed me outta my uniform?"

"The nurses did, honey," said Eleanor.

"Well it's a good thing I was wearin' my new knickers."

The doctor told Chip his head might be sore for a few days, but Chip was still puzzled and unsettled, refusing to accept an aspect of his injury that went beyond the knowledge of anyone in the room. He wanted to know where he had been for the last several hours. Just where was he that made his recollection so fuzzy?

"Well, Chip," said the doctor, "you were in a long, deep sleep."

"Is that what it is to not be conscious?"

"Well, yes...sort of. You are simply not engaged to anything going on around you. You are not awake and you cannot be awakened because your body experienced a shock –"

"Then why did I hear you say it was an honor for you to have me here in your hospital?" said Chip.

"You heard that?"

"I sure did. I felt like I was risin' outta my skin when I heard that. So *when* did my conscience go n' just where did it go off to without my permission? And if it did go away, how come when it come back it wasn't damaged goods?"

"Chip," said his sister Norma, "it is as though you were separated from this reality for a little while – as if you were separated from us without realizing it. You don't necessarily give *permission*."

"It's called, The Hereafter!" said Ring Lardner, coming into the room. "Hiya, Chipper!"

"This is the man that got a doctor for you," said Matty.

"Glad to see you are up and awake," said Lardner.

"Nice to see you, Mr. Lardner. I've got a bit of a headache, but I feel fine enough to haul a few bales of wet hay."

"I am doing a story on you, pal, and this is one of the finest finishes a writer could ask for."

Ring Lardner, Chip Doolin and the others, carried on about baseball, *The Hereafter* and the bump on his head. Chip's questions about the conscience were never answered to his liking, and it sparked an urge to research the matter on his own, which he vowed to do as soon as he had the time. You see, as Chip grew older, wisdom, learning and the workings of the mind became cherished assets to him, he knew that locked within them were the secrets to life, and it was the only way to grow from within.

"Did we end up winnin' that doggone windy game?" asked Chip.

"No," said Jennings, putting his hand on Chip's shoulder, "but we didn't lose it neither. I don't know if we're to continue it at some date or leave it as it was. You made the last play – and it was one of the finest catches I ever seen. You got lots o' guts, kid, and I sure am glad you're on my side.

When Chip left the hospital, some of the fans from the ballpark were still waiting outside to see him. He paused to sign some autographs and shake the hands of well-wishers, before giving a final wave and boarding a jitney to the next train.

Danger and The Dame Who Came Callin'

There exists a certain brand of women that take a special fancy to only ballplayers. It has been my experience that some of these particular gals are simply cracked, the most unstable birds you have ever seen. They are the sort that go out of their way to try and meet the ballplayers. You know...the normal, zany antics like sneaking into their hotel rooms, hiding in closets or under their beds, or downright stalking them. They live with a fantastic notion, infatuated with a vision or dream, wearing a virtual "BUYER BEWARE" label on their foreheads.

I have discovered that their behavior has a lot to do with their dream of being in the spotlight, or being married to someone who is. The prospect is especially enticing considering these are men who stay in shape from playing a boy's game *and* get paid to do it; two elements that tantalize this brand of women, tantalizes their psyche and is seen as an instant opportunity to leave the poor house or get some attention or...maybe even be part of a scandal that ends up on the front page of the newspaper.

"Oh, how that Doolin whacks that ball! My, he must be a charmer!" said Gracie Galloway, the roused daughter of a real estate pioneer.

When a ballplayer reaches the Big Leagues, it is called, "The Big Show". Part of Gracie's dream was to be part of that show. An ex-boyfriend called her a gold digger, to which Gracie replied, "No, I just like diggin' for gold. Besides, if you hadn't got cut by the White Sox, you'd still have me."

Gracie's fascinations had shifted to Chip Doolin. She wanted to be his girl in the biggest way, so obsessed in fact, that when the Tigers traveled all the way to Washington for a three game road series, Gracie made the trip too, following right along. It was her boldest move yet, and her aim was to make her affection known.

"Oooh, that Chipper, he's been makin' good," she said to her friend, Patty, who made the trip with her. "He's breakin' all the homer records! Why he's bound to be oozin' in fame. And I wanna brush myself against'em so I can have that fame too. I just can't wait – "

"Isn't that boy married?" asked Patty.

"Well, he sure as heck may be married, but I expect all that to change as soon as he lays those naïve eyes of his on me," said Gracie, brushing a curly strand of red hair from her face. Her lips were full and sensuous, and her cheeks were perky and rouged. She was certainly an attractive gal, but she looked the role she played. Her energy and aura reeked with hidden motive, and it colored her persona.

"I'm gonna walk right up to him, Patty. I sure am. As soon as we get off this train, I'm gonna walk right up to'em, rub my bosom against'em and steal'em away."

⚾ ⚾ ⚾

When Walter Johnson saw Chip warming up on the field, the kind fellow nicknamed, "The Big Train", because of his pitching prowess, came over to congratulate Chip on his success at the big league level.

In the latter part of 1909, Johnson's Washington club was still languishing in the cellar of the division, hardly able to average a run per game, while Chip's Tiger club was still flourishing in first place.

"Thank you, Walter. When you come to Detroit, I'd be thrilled to have you meet my nephew. His name is Walter too! And what a feisty lil' kid is he – full o' pee and vin-gar."

"I'd be much obliged –" started Walter.

"Chipper! Oh, Chipper darlin', over here!"

As soon as I heard her from where I was sitting in the dugout, I knew there was trouble.

Walking onto the field toward Chip, waving her arms with a smile pasted across her face was none other than Gracie Galloway, the flaming redhead with a penchant for havoc. Walter politely excused himself while all of Chip's Tiger mates stopped what they were doing to watch the buxom and vivacious Gracie walk – or rather traipse across the field.

"Chipper never told us he knew a girl like that. I'll have to have a word with that boy," said Germany Schaefer.

Gracie approached Chip and without a moment's hesitation, in flowing stride, she wrapped her arms around his neck and seductively looked into his eyes. The press and newspaper boys immediately scrambled for their pads.

"Oh, no...hold on, boys," said Jennings with caution. "Don't you dare let that ink out just yet," but before he could stop him, a cameraman quickly set up and snapped a picture. "Hey! Get the hell outta here!" said Jennings, climbing the steps of the dugout and chasing him off.

After several minutes Gracie still had her arms around Chip. His teammates started to make slow passes, trying to eavesdrop on what Gracie was saying – she was the only one doing the talking.

"Oh, go ahead, you can put your arms around

me, it's okay. Oh, your muscles! My! You're in grand shape, and you get paid for it! Why Mr. Doolin, you're a Big League star and I like that. You need someone who appreciates that. And you are just the handsomest thing I ever did see. I'm a single woman, and I want you to be my beau. Do you like the color of my lipstick? I wore it just for you."

Back in the dugout, Jennings was squirming. "Hey, Donie," he said, "what's comin' off over there?"

Well, Hughie...she's seducin' the heck outta him, and I don't even think he knows her. I think she's got'em scared stiff. I'm fixin' to go and break it up myself, try to save the kid –"

"No, no, allow me that honor. I think it's best if I save ole' Chipper. Nope, I don't reckon he knows that girl from a piece o' bubble gum. Just look at his face. White as a ghost."

I watched the dignified Jennings climb the dugout steps and make his way over.

"So why don't you take me out dancin' tonight, Chipper. Then we can go somewhere quiet, just you and me. Pick me up at seven darlin' and I'll be wearin' nothin' but –"

"Pardon me, ma'am, but who are you? Cuz I know he don't know who you are."

"Well, of course he knows me, don't you Chipper?" said Gracie, before smacking a wet kiss on his cheek.

Chipper was stunned into silence. *Total* silence. A doctor may have even surmised that he had submerged into a catatonic state.

"See?" said Jennings. "He don't know you. Now who in the devil are ya? Cuz I'm onto you."

"Oh, you are, are you? I do believe this doesn't concern you. It concerns me and Chipper, and this is not any way to treat a lady –"

"It certainly does concern me. He's my ballplayer and you ain't no lady. A real lady's got more class than you. Now I'm gonna ask you to leave or I can have you removed –"

"Well," said Gracie, elevating her chin, "I happen to be the daughter of a pioneer."

"Oh? What type is that?"

"Real estate. He bought real estate in Hollywoodland. Probably beyond your knowledge –"

"Well, this ain't your property and *that*," said Jennings, pointing to Chip, "certainly *is* my knowledge. Now beat it! And stay away from my ballplayer."

Gracie reluctantly left the field in the same strutting manner she had come onto it, huffing and puffing along the way. She was clearly peeved at being shown up by Jennings in such a way, and a woman as dangerous as that, we all knew, was already plotting her next move.

It took a while to snap Chip out of his trance. Rossman had to start in his place before Chip took over in the fourth inning. He went hitless in three at-bats with three strikeouts, as the Tigers suffered a rare 2-1 loss.

Jennings warned Chip after the game to keep an eye over his shoulder. He told him that the woman was a "poison pill", and likely to spring up anywhere without notice.

Later that evening, Chip had dinner with Matty McIntyre and Donie Bush in the hotel restaurant. Matty and Donie roomed together whenever the team traveled. Chip hadn't a roommate because of his incessant and often boisterous snoring that was rumored to be so loud, the window shades fluttered – but that was an account given by a bush leaguer who spent just a week with the Tiger club before being cut, and he must have been so darned tired that he imagined the shades moving, enveloping and closing on his brief playing career.

"Well, Chipper, I'll tell ya somethin' from mine own experience," said Bush. "I bet under this dame Gracie's clothes, she has herself a ripped girdle."

"Huh?"

"Her girdle, Chipper. I'm sayin' it's ripped n' torn

beneath her clothes."

"You really think so, Donie?" said Matty.

"Sure, on top she looks elegant n' such, like some fine man's daughter, but beneath I bet she's poor as a hog and has the manners of a cock-a-roach. I bet her girdle's torn – but you ain't the one to find out," said Bush, pointing a finger at Chip.

"And I don't wanna find out. And on that note, I'm gonna head up n' get me some rest. Lord knows I need it after whiffin' thrice today," said Chip.

"Thrice?"

"Aww, shucks, Donie! C'mon, that's Norma's doin'. She's tryin' to get me all talkin' funny. She was readin' Shakespeare at dinner the other night –"

"Yes, she's quite the lady, ain't she?" said Matty.

"Matty's gone n' lost his head over your sister, Chipper. He's all goo goo. He talks in his sleep every night now, and you don't wanna know what he's been sayin'. It would make even sir Shakespeare blush."

Chip slid the key into the hotel room door, turned the handle and entered. The room was dark and shadowy. There was a collision of scents – of fresh linen, new paint, and that transient mustiness that old hotels have. A window was open that he did not recall opening, but he accepted it as part of the bewilderment that had marked the day, and thought nothing of it.

The sounds of galloping horses echoed outside when Chip raised the flame in the oil lamp near the bed. As the flame rose, so did the shadows, crawling and scaling the yellowish walls in concert, like bedtime spirits; hollow and weary, the shadows outfitted forms and figures and mystical creatures that seemed to have a pulse all their own. One of the more dominant shadows proved not to be a shadow at all, but the real, vital visage of Gracie Galloway. She was quietly sitting in the wing chair, in the corner of the room, with her legs crossed.

Chip later described it as a scary scene plucked from the pages of a radio play, and he nearly jumped through his skin at the site of her, whacking his head against the wall, while Gracie remained still, looking evilly upon her victim.

"I don't give a damn if you hurt that big head of yours. Maybe it will knock some sense into you. I want you and I'm going to have you, and that's that. You're my prize and I deserve it. Besides, I'm a real estate pioneer's daughter. How's that for a dowry?"

Chip was uncertain of his next move. "I'm not one o' them unclean men," he said. "I've already taken the vows to the woman that has my heart. And I love her. You're a mighty pretty gal n' all – you sure are. But you ain't – "

"Shut up!" said Gracie, rising in anger and slamming her fist into the wall. "Now you look here. You're gonna leave that woman and you're takin' me, or you ain't gonna play ball again!" She drew a jackknife from her skirt pocket and unfolded a four-inch blade. With her other hand, she popped a pill in her mouth and swallowed hard.

"Are – are you a crazy?" said Chip.

"I'll show you crazy, you dumb country boy. You're marryin' me – "

"I can't do that. I – I already got me a wife and like I say, I love her. Now please put that away –"

"Be quiet! The only word you'll answer is "yes". Or I'll put you in the worst slump of your short career."

"I'm sorry you gone and got yourself all upset, but I can't –"

"Yes you will!" said Gracie, moving closer to Chip with the knife pointed straight at him. "*You* made me upset. You couldn't just kiss me on the field today could you? You couldn't just make *believe* you knew me, could you? You silly idiot –"

"Now no one calls me such a name!"

Gracie squeezed the handle of the knife and cornered Chip between the bed and the wall. The blade gleamed under the light from the oil lamp. The knifepoint was now inches from Chip's abdomen. She took joy in the fear on Chipper's face, faking thrusts into his side and laughing out loud. "I can call you an idiot if I want to," she said, raising her voice. "You silly idiot! You're marryin' me and –"

"Oh, no he ain't!" said Hughie Jennings, rushing into the room, followed by two uniformed policemen and half the Tiger team.

Both officers drew their guns when they saw Gracie holding the knife.

"But I'm Gracie Gallagher, daughter of a gold pioneer."

"I thought it was real estate in California," said Jennings.

Gracie turned the knife on herself. Plunged. And that was all. She fell weakly, bouncing off the corner of the bed and onto the floor, amid gasps from the onlookers. When her arm flailed back, her blouse rose above her hips revealing a tattered and torn girdle. Only a trickle of blood fell from the blade. She was quickly taken to the hospital.

Jennings remained undaunted. "That coward," he said, after the commotion had settled, "that phony coward –"

"No, Hughie..." said Chip, "she was just a sick woman. She needs help and some hope, is all. I ain't so sure you could blame a person for that."

"And you can't save 'em neither. For your sake, Chipper, I'm just glad you're safe. I had a hunch she'd be back, and when I heard that thump on the side o' the wall, I knew somethin' was up. But don't be feelin' too bad for that dame. She was a poison pill. My Mama always told me, "saviors get slaughtered and martyrs get punished." So don't you try to be neither one. You can get hurt plenty by a dame like that. I seen it many times," said Jennings.

The eventual fate of Gracie Galloway went unknown, although months later, one of the men on the Tiger club saw a lady that looked strikingly similar. He saw her photo in the newspaper, under the *Wedding Announcements*:

> *Gracie Seymour and Bobby Seymour were married today. The groom is a professional golfer. The bride, formerly Gracie Gwenlin, is the daughter of a fashion pioneer.*

There exists a certain brand of women that take a special fancy to only ballplayers – and then there are those women that underestimate the heart of a married man.

Walter Meets Walter

When the Washington Nationals came to Detroit to play the Tigers in a four-game weekend series – which included a Sunday doubleheader – Chip invited Walter Johnson to his home in the suburbs for a four-course dinner and an evening of relaxation.

Walter Perry Johnson, the strapping six foot one inch hurler was known for his fast one. His superlatives were already legendary. There were some hitters who did not even wait for their third strike – instead they strolled back to the dugout after just two because they knew they would fail to connect against him, or simply because they feared they might get hit by one of his fastballs, since Walter could occasionally unleash a wild one. The umpires enjoyed seeing this occur, because it sped up the game. You may be asking yourself, 'Who would give up a third strike?' But they did, and I saw it happen. Walter was one of the first modern day hurlers to put fear into the opposing hitters. Johnson would drown the hitter's confidence with his imposing, sweeping delivery – the kick of the long leg and the whip of the arm – and then that fastball, so fast that some hitters claimed to have never seen it blow past them, and still others reported seeing just a blur and hearing a WHOOSH!

Earlier in the day Johnson shut out the Tigers, 1-0, en route to his seventh victory of the season. He would have had more victories if his club scored more runs for him, but since they could hardly hit a ball even if it wasn't moving, Johnson was suffering through a season with more losses than what he should have had. If he failed to limit the opposition to two runs or less, his chances of winning were virtually less than sneezing once a week. But on this day, he limited Detroit to just three hits – one was a double by Doolin – and he struck out ten Tigers, which included Matty McIntyre three times.

Besides being dubbed "The Big Train", Johnson also carried the nickname of "The Big Swede".

"So why do they call you that?"

"I'm sorry Matty, why do they call me what?"

"The fellas from your bench and the reporters. They call you, "The Big Swede"."

"Oh," said Walter, smiling shyly, "because they think I'm Swedish."

"And ain't you then? It does seem you got blonde

in that head o' yours."

"No, I am not."

"You're not?"

"No."

"Why?"

"Why am I not Swedish?"

"Why don't you tell them boys you ain't?"

"Matty!" said Norma Doolin, "It is "those" boys. 'Why do you not tell *those* boys' –"

"Oh, alright! Please!" said Matty, waving his hand in frustration.

"Hey, Matty," said Chip, "you sore 'bout somethin'?"

"Sore? What would I be sore about? I wanna know why he don't tell'em he ain't Swedish –"

"And there is not such a word –"

"Norma, shut up!" said Matty.

As if on cue, Chip instantly rose from his seat. A tense but terse silence intervened. Norma shifted in her chair, visibly hurt by the outburst. Matty only lowered his head, immediately aware of the wrong he had just committed.

"There's nobody that talks to my sister or any woman like that, and tells her to do such a thing. You announce love for my sister and yet you speak to her in such a way?" said Chip, retaining a calm and even tone. "I will not stand for it and I think you need to spend some alone time with yourself, so please leave my home. You seem to be confusin' your sour attitude toward the game of baseball with the game of life, just cuz you didn't fair so well on this day. Three strikeouts may be somethin' to be sore at, but it don't give you the right to be mean to others. Now you go dine by yourself and think on it."

Matty slowly rose from his chair. He replaced his still folded napkin and put it back on the plate. He tucked in his chair, and silently made his way to the door.

"Matty," said Walter, "I don't tell them I'm not Swedish because I have friends who are Swedish, and I wouldn't want to offend them."

Matty McIntyre only nodded his head, saddened and dejected over his own behavior and antics. "I'm sorry, Norma," he solemnly said, before leaving.

⚾ ⚾ ⚾

Following dinner, with the wholesome smells of cooked chicken and candied plums still lingering, Norma, Eleanor and Chip thought it was time for Walter to meet Walter.

"I'll go wake him," said Norma, scurrying up the stairs.

Little Walter was not yet two winters old, but he possessed the energy of a windmill, wild with animation, especially after a long nap. He was a fiery-eyed little boy, but disciplined under Norma's watchful eye.

"Mr. Johnson," said Norma, coming into the room, "this is my son, Walter. Chip calls him, "The Little Train", after you."

Walter Johnson took 'The Little Train' in his arms and held him high over his head. "What a fine child, Norma," said Johnson.

"Elly, darlin'?" said Chip, "Do you need any help in there with makin' that frosted cake?"

"No, thank you sweetheart. If I let you, I know the frosting will never make it to the cake."

The elder Johnson reached into a satchel he had brought and pulled out an autographed baseball, specially inscribed, *To Little Walter, may all your wishes come true. Sincerely, Walter Johnson.* The boy needed both hands to grasp the ball, but he was fascinated at the sight of his own name written twice.

"Oh my!" cried Eleanor from the kitchen.

"What is it, Elly?" said Chip.

"I think my ring fell down the sink!"

Well, as I am sure you can imagine, that blunt announcement quickly changed the tone of the occasion. Within a few moments, Chip, Walter and Eleanor were all taking turns looking and reaching into the sink.

They tried to locate the ring – the diamond that Chip had given her when he proposed marriage – but the efforts were futile, and so, they decided to dismantle the sink and the plumbing, pipe by pipe.

More than two hours transpired without success. Finally Chip and Walter, with grease-covered hands, decided they had better put the sink back together because either the ring was never there to begin with, or it was by now, on its way to settling in one of the Great Lakes of Michigan.

"Elly, honey, we've looked in every darn pipe there is here."

"Chip," said Walter, "did this pipe go here or did that one?"

"Well, I reckon that one don't fit here so –"

"But I took the first pipe I removed and put it here."

"Oh, no I moved that one cuz I thought it went under here –"

"No, this pipe here goes there –"

"But I thought that one connected to the sink –"

"Well...now you may be right, but no –"

"Where's the curly pipe?" said Chip.

"Chipper, there are two curly pipes," said Walter.

"Umm...pardon me, but Chip? Walter? No, not you, honey, I mean, Mr. Johnson –"

Both men looked up at Norma from where they

THE ADVENTURES OF CHIP DOOLIN

sat on the floor, hands dirtied, faces smeared in places, grime on their clothes...

"Let's keep this simple. I only see six pipes," she said, taking charge, "and the two curly ones go in the middle –"

"Oh, I'm so sorry! I'm so, so sorry," cried Eleanor. "Honey, I lost our ring...and ruined Walter's night! What have I done?"

When Little Walter heard his name come from Auntie Eleanor's crying mouth, he also began to cry.

Norma comforted Little Walter, and Chip comforted Eleanor, while Big Walter put the sink back together.

⚾ ⚾ ⚾

It was well past the hour for dessert when they all sat down at the table for cake.

"Really Eleanor, it was no trouble at all. I'm having a swell time –"

"Why don't you sleep here, Walter, and we can take the train to the ballpark together tomorrow. Joe Cantillon is in the know that you're with me."

"I suppose that would be a fine idea. Thank you."

"Great, it's settled," said Chip. "Let's eat, cuz this here frostin' looks good enough to swim in!"

Now I wasn't there for this one, but when Chip told me about it, I could not help but have fixed visions and pictures of the scene. After the first bite or two of Eleanor's cake, pleasantries and compliments on how darn good that cake was, went around the table. It may have been on the third or fourth mouthful when Chip experienced an odd sensation.

"Ouch!" exclaimed Chip, speaking out the side of his mouth. "Oh, Elly, I think I bit somethin' hard – sharp n' hard – what the devil..."

Whatever it was, Chip spit it into his hand. It came out in a pasty, white glob.

"Ewww, Chipper excuse yourself –"

"Norma, doggone it, hold on! Before I excuse myself, I need to know what I'm excusin' myself from. It may not be a legimate excusal."

"Le*git*imate, a legitimate excusal," said Norma.

"Yes, whatever you said."

In his lap, under the table, Chip took his napkin and wiped the object clean. "Hmmm..."

"What is it?" asked Norma.

"Yes Chip, what is it? Is it a piece of spoon or something?" said Elly. "I just can't do anything right tonight – a complete disaster I am!"

Chip took his time surveying and wiping the object, taking pleasure in raising the suspense, as a wry smile crossed his face.

"Chipper Doolin," said Norma, "we are going to

leap through the roof if you don't tell us –"

"My, my, it sure does have a pretty shine. And that specialness is still in the center. Why, Elly darlin'...my symbol o' love to you was in my sweet tastin' frostin'. It's your ring, sweetheart!"

Chip knelt down beside Elly's chair and slid the ring back onto her finger, and while applause and laughter rang throughout the house, suddenly, Little Walter wound up and threw the ball square across the table, where Big Walter caught it.

"What an arm on that boy!" said Chip.

"Yes! Yes! Yes, but..." said Norma, "he's not supposed to throw things at the dinner table."

"But what a throw!" said Big Walter. "That ball had some speed on it!"

There was a knock at the door.

Chip got out of his chair to answer it. When he swung the door open, there was a sheepish-looking Matty McIntyre, holding a bouquet of colored flowers and a box of chocolates.

"Hiya, Chip. I'm mighty sorry. I thought on it like you say, and I'm sorry for bein' such a poor sport. The chocolates are for you and Elly, and the flowers are for Norma if – if she'll still see me."

Chip turned to his sister, who gave a nod of approval.

"C'mon in, pal. You're just in time for cake."

Brawlin'

Detroit was in Boston to face the feisty Red Sox in a decisive four-game series. Boston was red hot, having won seven straight games and fifteen of their last eighteen, to pull within three games of the first place Tigers, with less than two months to play in the season.

It was that time of the year when the teams at the top of the division start to fantasize about their chances for the World Series, and the big cash bonus that would come, just for getting there.

Tensions were high on both sides. The Tigers *had* to hold off the Red Sox. In game one, before a capacity crowd at the Huntington Avenue ball field, they were sending their ace to the mound, George Mullin.

Boston was countering with right-handed Eddie Cicotte, who was also slated to start the fourth game of the series. It was the same Eddie Cicotte who would later be banned from baseball, implicated in

THE ADVENTURES OF CHIP DOOLIN

the 1919 Chicago Black Sox scandal.

It was a humid day in Boston and most of the men in the stands already had to replace their collars with one freshly starched, as the collars they had put on earlier in the morning, had already wilted and curled under the wet humidity that filled the air. It was so muggy and wet in fact, that clothes left out to dry on clotheslines were not drying at all and had to be brought indoors and hand wrung from the dampness. Dogs were lazy and cats were antsy, but every mortal in Boston was ready for a ballgame.

"Hey, Chipper," said Germany Schaefer, "there's a champion in the front row that'd like to meet you."

"A champion?" said Chip.

"Sure is. A champion pugilist."

"A what?"

"Ain't you never heard of a pugilist?"

"Ain't that a dog?"

"No, that's a Pug, spelled P-U-G."

"Gee, I'm sorry, Germany," said Chip with a forlorn look, "but I ain't never heard o' no –"

"Aww, alright! You don't have to go and start feelin' all bad on me just cuz you ain't heard o' no pugilist. It's a boxer, Chipper. A prize fighter. Ain't you never boxed before?"

"Well, my Daddy taught me how to fight, but I ain't never been in no fight before, for reals."

"Chip, sometimes I think you're more innocent than a brand new baby," said Germany.

"Well, ain't they innocent to begin with?"

"That there's my point."

"Well, that's a lousy point –"

"Do you wanna meet this boxin' champ or dontcha?"

"Well, if you'll doggone tell me who the devil it is!"

"Hey, boys!" said George Moriarty, rushing into the dugout. "Did you see John L. Sullivan in the front row?"

"That's what I been tryin' to tell Chipper here –"

"Germany, why didn't you just tell me his name, instead o' all this pug-list stuff. I know who John L. Sullivan is!" said Chip, before running up the steps to go meet the great and famed boxer.

John L. Sullivan, the last of the bare-knuckle champions, was arguably the best heavyweight fighter of all time. He signified the end of the bare-knuckle boxing era. His 1889 fight with Jake Kilrain, which lasted seventy-five rounds, was boxing history's last bare-knuckle heavyweight match. Sullivan is responsible for helping to usher in a significant transformation – the use of gloves in professional fighting.

The broad-shouldered Sullivan, at fifty years old, had retired from the professional boxing circuit and

THE ADVENTURES OF CHIP DOOLIN

on this day, was seated in the front row donning a fedora and eating roasted peanuts, occasionally pausing to stroke his long, sloping moustache that stretched across his face.

"I've heard plenty about you, Doolin, and I wanted to meet you," said Sullivan, in a thick Irish brogue.

"Thank you, sir. It's an absolute honor to meet you."

"Say, you've got a firm grip there!" said Sullivan, after shaking hands with Chip. "I like that! Tells me you're not only sincere, but strong too. You ever box before?"

"Only with my Daddy."

"I'm sure you've got a good left punch."

"That's a mighty large compliment from your own mouth, Mr. Sullivan. Thank you!" said Chip, who spent the remainder of his pre-game warm-up time chatting with John L. Sullivan and listening to the champ's advice on life and accounts of his boxing feats. His storied career inspired and impressed Chip.

"I remember my Daddy always telling me stories about you, Mr. Sullivan. And he'd always end them stories in a poetic-like way: "Make sure you be a man just like John. L. Sullivan." So I can't tell ya how happy I am to meet you, and I can't wait to tell my Daddy."

"How would you like me to write your Pop a short letter, and I'll sign my name to it?"

"Oh, Mr. Sullivan, that'd be just the swellest thing in the world. He'd be overjoyed."

Chip shook hands once more with John L. Sullivan, and the two men made plans to meet again after the game. Sullivan was a real charismatic gentleman. An imposing figure whose huge hands dwarfed most men's. Little did he or any fan know, that on this day, they'd all be in for a real fighting treat.

⚾ ⚾ ⚾

The first pitch of the ball game to leadoff hitter Donie Bush was much too close for comfort, and it was the tone of events to come.

Players barked from the Tiger bench in protest, and in response, Cicotte's next pitch was more of the same – up and in on Bush, this time sending him flailing back.

Cicotte smirked toward the Tiger bench before throwing three straight strikes, striking out Bush with a fastball that nicked the outside corner.

The next hitter was Cobb, who yelled out to Cicotte, "Try throwin' one o' them high n' tight ones to me and you'll be wearin' my spike on your cheek!"

Cicotte pitched carefully to the dangerous Cobb, who lined out to third for the second out of the inning.

Chip Doolin then walked slowly to the plate. He dug his back spike into the dirt, but before he could get set, Cicotte threw one right at Chipper's bean. He saw it coming just in time to duck out of the way.

"Hey now cut that out!" said Doolin, pointing the barrel of the bat at Cicotte in a rare burst of anger, with Chipper's well-defined forearms tensing. "That's about enough o' that!"

"Calm down, Chipper," said Carrigan, the Boston catcher.

"Don't tell me to calm down, tell your pitcher to calm down cuz I got me a bat in my hand, and if you call another pitch like that Mr. Carrigan, I'm sorry but I'm gonna have to bust your jaw and break it to pieces all over home plate."

All of the Tiger players were now yelling at Cicotte from the bench, anxious to take some swings at him.

John L. Sullivan heard the whole exchange from the front row and yelled to Doolin, "Chipper, don't apologize, if that dirty chap does it again, just slug'em one!"

"So you got the retired champion on your side, do ya – " said Carrigan.

"I'm gonna un-retire if I have to come outta this here seat after you, Carrigan," yelled Sullivan.

Carrigan shut his mouth and got back down into his crouch, behind the plate.

Cicotte's next pitch was a fast one. Doolin unleashed his anger and hit a bullet right back through the box, sending Cicotte to the ground to avoid being hit.

Chip's Tiger mates cheered. "You better duck," said Crawford, walking up to the plate, "less your fat head come off."

Doolin's hit rattled and frustrated Cicotte, who slapped his glove against his hip and carelessly straightened his cap, mumbling profanities all the while.

As Jake Stahl – the Boston first sacker – was holding Doolin on at first, he gave Chip a firm elbow in the ribs. Chip promptly shoved Stahl to the ground in one swift motion, and the capacity crowd rose to their feet. Both benches emptied and the players came onto the field ready to brawl.

Stahl scampered to get up, as umpire Bill Klem came out from behind home plate to intervene.

"Why'd you shove me?" said Stahl.

"Why'd you elbow me, you no good, dirty, hog washin', dung smellin', rat lovin', swashbucklin' yellow-bellied barn worm?"

The players on the field all looked at Chip in mild

amazement following his barrage of name-calling.

"Well now, Chipper, those are some – some fine words you have there for uh, Mr. Stahl," said Klem.

"They sure are Chipper, you sure did tell'em," said Donie Bush. "Way to go! I don't think I could of thought of them words."

"Heck, on my worst day I don't recall ever hearin' one o' them words from my wife when she starts on me," said Stanage. "*barn worm* was by far my personal favorite."

Chip's name-calling unintentionally served as an intercept and diffused the tense moment on the field.

"Why he's lucky I don't –" started Chip.

"Alright, alright," said Klem, "now this is going to stop right here and now. The next troublemaker gets a ticket on the next train. Now Mr. Stahl, I suspect you had to do something to get Chipper this upset, and I don't even want to hear what you have to say. I want it to stop right now – not to mention that he knocked you to the ground like you were a match stick! So, let's go, boys. Play ball!"

When play resumed, the Tigers reached Cicotte for three consecutive singles to take a 2-0 lead.

In the seventh inning, with the Tigers leading 3-0, Cicotte was set to come to bat and lead off for the Red Sox. Mullin had so far limited the Boston bunch to just three hits – two of them by Tris

Speaker. While he was pitching exceptionally well, he had not forgotten Cicotte's antics in the first inning. Mullin waited patiently and chose his time to get even for his Tiger mates.

Mullin's first three pitches to Cicotte, were all on the outside part of the plate, two of them good enough for strikes. Cicotte moved in closer to the plate, expecting another outside pitch. Mullin stared in for the sign from Stanage. Then he rocked, wound and threw his best fastball of the day, aimed straight at Cicotte, who could do nothing more than turn away from it, and the ball struck him square in the back with a hollow THUMP!

Cicotte winced in pain. He spun back around and glared at Mullin.

"Take your base, Eddie!" said umpire Klem, but Cicotte remained in the batter's box. "I said, 'TAKE YOUR BASE'!"

The beanball war was on and everyone now knew there were more fireworks to come. The fans throughout the park were buzzing.

Cicotte took his time jogging down to first base, hoping to catch the eye of Mullin, who continued to purposely ignore him. With nowhere to vent his anger, Cicotte once again turned his attention to Doolin, who was standing on the first base bag.

Cicotte suddenly went from a jog to a run – charging with aggression, his arms pumping at full speed, right at Doolin. Chip side-stepped him but Cicotte managed to drive his spikes into Chip's foot, giving him a hard bruise, from which Chip instantly smarted and buckled, falling to one knee.

The benches cleared and an all-out battle of fisticuffs commenced. The Tigers and Red Sox met at mid-field and slugged it out, punches flying everywhere. Bodies fell from blows and blood spattered from broken noses and cut lips. When I looked out across the infield, I saw gobs of blood flying through the air, body blows and face jabs.

Chip had since gotten back up on his feet and instead of swinging the muscular lefty was literally *throwing* Red Sox players to the ground.

Suddenly, Chip looked right and saw Cicotte charging him once again, eyes blazing in a fit of fury. Just then, John L. Sullivan stepped between them, and the five foot nine inch Cicotte bounced off the champion's chest and fell to the ground.

When the rest of the brawling players saw Sullivan on the field, in a measure of respect *and* fear, the melee abruptly halted.

"Now hear me!" said the burly Sullivan, his voice carrying throughout the park. He pointed to Cicotte, "You want to fight this here Doolin, do ya? Okay. I'm presidin' here. Now make a circle round, boys. C'mon."

The players on both teams formed a human

boxing ring, gathering shoulder-to-shoulder, blood-stained shirt to blood-stained shirt.

"Now the first man to put the other one down on the ground wins! Then you shake hands and it's over. They'll only be one round in this here fight – go at it until a man falls," said Sullivan, who turned to Chip and quietly advised him, "Hit'em first and hit'em hard."

The crowd grew silent. Some of the fans exchanged bets and waved cash, as if it were a prizefight. Sullivan stayed between the two men and kept them apart until he was ready.

"I want a good, clean fight," said Sullivan, before announcing, "On your marks! Get set! And there's the bell!"

Sullivan quickly drew two paces back, and Cicotte and Doolin began circling and calculating like two practiced boxers. The fans inside Huntington Park roared and screamed with great fervor, and the event gave me and all the other press boys one great story to write.

Chip's face turned a slow red. His jaw was firm; his muscles taut and his large, farm boy fists clenched. He lowered his body into a slight crouch, and his hands rose like a boxer, to protect the side of his temple and chin.

Then, in one dynamic burst, Chip stepped with his right and threw a power-packed left that landed

square on Cicotte's nose, snapping his head back like a springboard, sending a spatter of blood into the air. Cicotte didn't even see it coming it was so fast. The awestruck pitcher fell in a heap to the ground – motionless.

Sullivan immediately stepped in and raised Chip's arm, and announced him as the victor. "I knew you had a good left punch! Atta boy, Chipper! A one punch knockout!"

Smelling salts were summoned to rouse Cicotte from his stupor, and when play finally resumed, a relief pitcher named, Charley "Sea Lion" Hall replaced him on the mound for the Red Sox.

When Cicotte came to, he was unsure whether it was night or day and questioned why he was wearing such funny-looking clothes, "and why'd you boys wake me from the wonderful dream I was havin'? I was flyin' through the sky!"

The Tigers went on to sweep the Red Sox convincingly in all four games. When Cicotte pitched the fourth game, not a single beanball was thrown and Chip Doolin hit two homers and a run-scoring double in the victory.

⚾ ⚾ ⚾

When Chip went into the clubhouse after that final game, between congratulatory handshakes, he was given a telegram that had just arrived from his sister Norma:

> Chipper. Brought Ellie to see doctor. Complained of stomach pain and nausea. Will let you know. Love Norma.

A Doolin Death

Death, like youth, is a season. Like the blooming and fading of life, it often blows in with suddenness, coming and going, passing expeditiously through, inconspicuous, like a soft night's breeze. With death, rides the precious meanings and nuances of life: the remembrances, the nostalgia, the regret, the yearning, the appreciation, the list of words unspoken and the hollow pains of loss. Just knowing they are no longer here on earth, sharing and witnessing the same life that you share and witness, is, in itself, enough to bring unshakable gloom.

Thomas Clarke Doolin, known to Chip as "Pa" or "Pop" or "Daddy"...died suddenly while plucking tomatoes from the vine on the family farm.

He had paused to eat one, said his grieving wife. *She* had paused while washing the dishes to look out the window. She paused when he paused to form a poignant, singular moment. In the midst of their pause, he fell. One last enduring image – the handkerchief sticking out of the back pocket of his overalls. In a sense, they died together, sharing the same pause, sharing one final moment – the same inhale and exhale, and for Thomas Clarke Doolin it was his last. He died with the tomato in his mouth, with the pulp and fresh, succulent juices running down his chin. Mrs. Doolin dropped the dish she was holding and it shattered in slow motion into a million pieces, a metaphor for the million moments they had shared in marriage. Time slowed. She said it seemed to take forever to reach him, but she got there. She held her husband in her arms and wept, said thank you and I love you. It was a death in the afternoon, the result of a massive heart attack. He was just fifty years old. "At least it was fast and painless," everyone agreed, "yes, at least it was fast and painless." As a mother is the anchor of a family, a father is the skipper who steers the family ship. Chipper was now without his skipper, moving alone in the world, but not without sacred memories of the day he made a bet with his father and sent a crab apple soaring across two farms, only to land at the feet of Eleanor. Chip now recalled the look on his father's face…his father's proud, delighted, awestruck, beautiful face…his father, grateful for every bit of him.

"Chip, are you ready? Do you have it memorized? Read it if you need to. Do you want to go over it again?" asked Norma.

"I think I – I got it, Norma. I just can't stop my dang hand from shakin'. Every time I try to fix my hair or wipe sweat off o' my brow, I hit myself in the face."

"Well, I know you will make *Daddy* proud, and I know he will be watching down from above."

The entire Detroit Tiger team was in attendance at the funeral, including the team owner, to pay their respects. Ring Lardner, Walter Johnson and I, along with a host of other prominent baseball personalities and journalists were also there, a direct testament to Chip, who was liked and respected by all.

"Thank ya'll for comin' to this here service," said Chip, to commence his eulogy. "My Daddy was a kind man, except for when my Mama was upset, and then he'd be cross n' moody, but that's because he loved my Mama n' hated to see her upset so. He always wanted to please everybody in his family n' I wanted to please him. I'm mighty glad he got to see me make good. Just a week before Daddy gone n' died, I had gone down to see'em on my off day. I had sent'em a telegram tellin'em I had got a surprise for'em. I met John L. Sullivan, the great prize fightin' champion as you all prob'ly read about that one in the papers. Well, I had for my Daddy a letter Mr.

Sullivan had written 'specially for my Daddy, with his name signed to it. He couldn't believe his eyes when I give it to'em. It was the happiest I had never seen'em. You see, Mr. Sullivan was a hero to my Daddy n' well, now that I come to thinkin' on it, my Daddy was my hero. He – he always...pardon me," said Chip, who had to pause to sip some water, but his hand shook so profusely, he spilled the water all over his suit. Norma stepped in and steadied his hand, grasping it around the glass firmly so he could drink. "Thank you, Norma. Uh...uh, my Daddy – I'm gonna miss my Pa."

Chip, his body trembling, reached inside his pocket and pulled out a piece of paper. He unfolded it, but his hand shook so much he could not read clearly what was written on the paper.

"My Daddy, he was a man who was a convict n' –"

"No! No! No!" said Norma in a heightened whisper, standing a few feet from him. "He was a man of conviction!"

"Oh! Daddy was – was many men of conviction. He stood up to the people for what he believed – aww, shucks! Ladies n' gentlemen I can't do no eul-gee. I'm just too darn broken up over my Daddy leavin' me. I'm gonna miss'em like heck n' that's all. He was my friend n' ally in this here crazy sorta life. I do know he always said when he died he wanted everyone to drink n' be merry. So after my lovin' sister Norma here says her kind words – and she says'em an awful lot better'n me! You oughtta hear her read Shakespeare n' such! So I'll give ya'll to her n' she can speak to you cuz after, I got some happy news to share with ya'll."

After Norma delivered a polished and eloquent eulogy, everyone gathered to partake in some light food, cold beer and Irish music, befitting an Irish funeral.

During the festive occasion designed to drown the sorrow, Chip and Eleanor found a solitary moment to walk back across the room, to the ornate wooden casket where Chip's father lay.

Chip wanted to stand beside his father again, to talk to him, and he wanted his wife with him. After Chip said a few heartfelt words – hoping he would see him again and how much he would miss him and how his favorite beer was a hit with the guests – he gave the casket a few taps as if he were patting a friend on the back. As soon as Chip finished tapping, suddenly, three mysterious taps were returned, seemingly coming from inside the coffin! Chip and Eleanor looked at each other in ghastly amazement. They stood frozen, unsure of what to do next.

"Chipper, honey," said Eleanor, "umm...tap it again, see what happens."

"Elly, why don't you tap it?"

THE ADVENTURES OF CHIP DOOLIN

"No, it worked for you. You do it."

"Elly it's – it's your turn to tap. I already done it –"

"No. You tap it, it's *your* father."

Chip gingerly reached across to tap the coffin, but before he could, three more taps came from inside.

"Elly! Elly! Holy Heaven! He beat me to it like he seen me!"

"Chip, I think we should get the doctor to open it and see."

"See what, Elly?"

"See – see who is tapping."

"Well, my doggone Daddy done the tappin'. Who else you think done it? Maybe he recollects an old song he wants to hear –"

"Chip, the Tiger team trainer is here, maybe he can do it."

"Let me try once more," said Chip, who got up enough courage to give three quick knocks on the coffin.

Elly and Chip waited for a response. One minute went by and then two, and each one that passed seemed to bring more color back into the faces of Chip and Eleanor, who were as white as flour.

"See Elly? It was nothin'," said Chip, after more than five minutes had passed without incident. "Let's go join the others and drink lots n' lots o' beer to fix our imaginations."

Just as they turned to leave, three bold knocks came from inside the coffin. Chip and Eleanor froze in their steps.

"Chip, you're hurting my hand. Let it go."

"Elly, go – go get that trainin' guy."

Before long, a rather jolly crowd had gathered around the coffin, with the Tiger team trainer, William Waldorf, standing in front of it. He had already drunk a few himself, making his nerve brazen and daring.

"I'm going to open the casket!" Waldorf announced to the gasping crowd. He chugged another beer for good luck, before lifting the lid.

When the casket opened, everything appeared normal. Thomas Clarke Doolin laid peacefully, one hand over the other, eyes closed.

"Now you say you knocked, Chipper?"

"That's right."

William Waldorf reached in and knocked three times on the inside of the casket. Everyone then waited in silence, gawking at the corpse. Then, after the passing of almost a minute, Pop Doolin's top hand rose three times, as if he were simulating painting the inside of the coffin.

Everyone present let out an "Ahhh!" Mrs. Doolin fainted and William Waldorf had another drink before checking for a pulse.

"Nothing. He's definitely, absolutely, positively

dead. What we have here is a case of reflex. You see, his nerves and sensory hardware are still intact and his body is merely responding as it normally would if he were alive. I've read this is quite a normal occurrence with the dead. I'm sorry everybody. This is probably Pop Doolin's way of wishin' he was here with us, maybe dancin' a Virginian jig."

The casket was re-sealed, Mrs. Doolin awoke, and the party resumed, much to Chip and Eleanor's relief, though they did have to change their undergarments that were soaked with perspiration and fright.

"Before ya'll leave on your way," Chip said to his friends and guests, "Elly and me would like to share some swell news. It's a sad day with my Daddy gone, so to make it even n' square, the happy news is Elly's pregnant! We's gonna have ourselves our first baby!"

A thunderous "Hooray" went up and rang throughout the hall. One by one they came up to congratulate Elly and Chip, and a new party began. More food and spirits were ordered and more music played, all in good cheer and merriment.

"It's a good thing we played our game early this mornin' before we came here," said Jennings to Crawford.

"And it's a good thing we play later in the day tomorrow, because we're gonna be here a whole while longer," said Crawford. "C'mon, let's eat some more before we catch that midnight train."

The Tigers won the morning game 5-1 that day, beating George Stallings' New York Club. Chip only thought it would be right if he played, because that is what his father would have told him to do. New York agreed to play early in the morning on account and in consideration of the wake, and all of the New York players offered their warm condolences.

Chip celebrated his father's memory with four hits in four at-bats, including another homer, before he and his teammates boarded the train to Virginia.

Weeks after the funeral, as time unfolded, it became evident that a new phase and cycle of life had begun to form in the Doolin family.

The farm was sold and bid a tearful farewell. Mama Doolin packed up what she needed and moved to Detroit, to live with Chip, Elly, Norma and Little Walter, with one in the oven. She had no sooner moved in, when Chip and Elly realized they needed to buy a bigger house, which they found just three streets from their existing home, on a street ironically named, "Thomas Clarke Boulevard". The entire Doolin family saw this as a good and fated omen.

Harmony resided in the household, harmony and love and laughter. Each new day buried the last, but memories never faded.

Chip endured through the gradual adjustment of life without his father. He found no other choice but to continue to engage in life, clipping along, resuming the pursuit of dreams and a worthy existence – one that mattered and one that brought pride, not only to himself but to his family. Chip found solace in living, preparing for a new addition to his family and his first immersion into fatherhood. Like his father, Chip Doolin persevered.

Death can be a reconciling of life, a catalyst for change, a time when old habits alter, and a reminder of all things temporary. Life is temporary, as are its moments; of pleasure; of ecstasy; of sadness; of humility; of loss. Thus, mourning, however devastating, is a temporary moment, for time does heal, and faith in this alone builds rainbows unseen until that one morning when you awake, and your heart is healed and the day is new; when the appreciation for life and living has expanded.

Godspeed to you, Thomas Clarke "Pop" Doolin. Godspeed to you, wherever your good spirit takes you.

The Series

The spirit of competition is good for a civilization. It instills discipline, courage, passion and occasionally, enough confidence to lift a world; it induces thoughts that spring from the zest and fervor of the moment. Senses are heightened and aroused, and the mind is more focused than usual, keenly aware of the stakes. Competition elicits feats of oneself previously thought unattainable, and it raises the bar of human performance and capability; it brings about the stuff of magic.

Back in the early days of the spring thaw, on the day Chip tried out for the Tigers – if you recall – after seeing Chip put on a hitting display, Ty Cobb approached him and said, *"Well Chip, keep hittin'em like that and we'll be goin' to the World Series again."* Ty was right. That 1909 World Series! It was a see-saw battle right up until the 7th game, and a great finale to the season, for all baseball fans.

It was the Tigers and the Pittsburgh Pirates. The

THE ADVENTURES OF CHIP DOOLIN

date for game one was October 8th, 1909. The crisp fall season had already begun to turn the color of the leaves, and many of the fans had already taken their wool clothes out of the wardrobe, having to don them on this chilly day.

The dangerous Pirates were stacked with talent, led by "The Flying Dutchman", shortstop Honus Wagner, and left fielder, Fred Clarke. Behind them was a strong supporting cast: Tommy Leach, Chief Wilson and Dots Miller. However, it was the pitching of the Pirates that was phenomenal. While most teams could boast of two or three top pitching arms, the Pirates had six! A young Babe Adams anchored the staff after coming on in the 2nd half of the season and posting an impressive 12-3 record, with an astonishing 1.11 ERA. He was followed by Howie Camnitz, who went 25-6 in the regular season; Vic Willis, who won 22 games that year, then Lefty Leifield, Nick Maddox and Deacon Phillippe.

Compared to the Tigers, the Pittsburgh pitchers were far more superior, and the Tiger club knew they had their hands full. All of the bookies had the Pirates winning in a short series. Never would they have believed it would go seven games...but it did!

The Pirates took game one, by the score of 4-1, helped by four Tiger errors that led to three unearned runs. The other Pirate run came on a solo home run by Fred Clarke. Babe Adams was the winning pitcher, going nine innings and scattering six hits, but Detroit's Mullin pitched nine of his own, and was the hard luck loser, his Tiger mates just played sloppy ball behind him. Catcher, Boss Schmidt, who was responsible for one of the errors, vowed not to kiss his wife again until after the series was over – needless to say, Mrs. Schmidt was not too happy about this news.

The Tigers roared back and took game two, walloping the Pirates and starter Howie Camnitz, by a score of 7-2, led by none other than Boss Schmidt, who drove in four of the runs with a single and a double. After seeing the success, now attributed to his abstinence from kissing, Mrs. Schmidt, needless to say, was even unhappier, putting her in a dour mood for the rest of the series. As revenge, she vowed not to cook for her husband for the rest of the series. "That's okay," Boss Schmidt said to one of the reporters, "I'll eat my glove if it means us winning the series." Doolin chipped in with a single and a run scored in the victory.

Game three came back to Detroit, where the Pirates staved off a late Tiger rally to take an 8-6 victory. Honus Wagner had three hits for the winners, while Donie Bush had four hits for the losers. Tiger starter Ed Summers lasted just one third of an inning and Boss Schmidt…went hitless and committed his second error of the series, which he promptly blamed on his wife not cooking for him. It was an accusation from which Mrs. Schmidt vowed to now lock him out of the house, "for tellin' all them reporters our private life, and bringin' them into our home!" she cried.

In the losing cause, Doolin jacked a monstrous two-run home run in the ninth inning that reached the moon. "Elly, I'm gonna lead my team to victory. I can feel it. I can *feel it*, I tell ya!" he said, following the game.

"Yes, you will darling...I can feel it too. You just keep on thinking that way. There's plenty of power in that confidence of yours."

In game four, the see-saw battle commenced, as the Tigers, behind brilliant pitching by George Mullin, blanked the Pirates 5-0. Lefty Leifield started for Pittsburgh, but was sent to the showers after just four innings in which he gave up five runs, all of them earned, despite six Pirate errors in the game. Mullin struck out 10 batters while yielding only five hits. It was just what the Tigers needed. Boss Schmidt was given the day off behind the plate due to exhaustion from a lack of sleep, and was replaced by Oscar Stanage. Mrs. Schmidt said that she would only let her husband back into the house – and into his bed – if he apologized and agreed to kiss her again. Boss declined with a simple comment: "Not if it means us losin' the series. I'd rather be sleepless and eat cardboard." After the game, his Tiger mates pitched in and bought him a four-course meal fit for a king. Doolin was relatively quiet at the plate, going 1 for 3 with a base hit.

Game five returned to Forbes Field, in Pittsburgh, where the Pirates, after scoring four runs in the seventh inning, went on to an 8-4 victory. Babe Adams won his second game of the series, while Ed Summers lost his second game. The game's highlight belonged to Fred Clarke, who homered with two men on base in the seventh inning, breaking a 3-3 deadlock. Chip Doolin went 2 for 4 with an RBI double, and Sam Crawford had three hits, for the Tigers. Boss Schmidt felt better, looked like a well-fed turkey, and fell asleep in the dugout, until he was awoken to replace Stanage behind the plate, in the 7th inning. After the game, he received a telegram from his wife:

> Don't you miss how I cook my chicken? And my apple pie? Don't you miss your bed? Don't you miss ME? I'll unlock the door if you come home when you get back to Detroit. Love, Your Mrs.

Game six was a 5-4 thriller, won by the Tigers at Bennett Park, to force that final game seven! George

Mullin was the pitching hero again, overcoming a first inning that saw the Pirates take a 3-0 lead, but the Tigers battled back, behind a two-run double by Chip Doolin. Mullin went the distance and Boss Schmidt, back in the starting lineup and back with his wife, went 1 for 3 with a walk.

"...but we ain't sleepin' in the same hay till the series is over! I'm sleepin' on the floor and that's that!" said Schmidt to his wife. She reluctantly agreed, made him some apple pie, and held his pinkie while they ate together at the dinner table.

Game seven...the first game seven, in the first World Series of Chip Doolin's young career, was nothing short of amazing. We all knew there would probably be more trips to the World Series – the fans, writers and I – but we also knew that this first one would be something special. It was strange in a way...we knew something momentous would occur, and it would surround Chip. That's what watching him play did; it made you *expect* something amazing every time he walked onto the ball field. When I saw a family of geese nesting in centerfield before the game, I wondered if Chip Doolin would have some mercy on the darling birds and not hit one out that way.

Through the first six games of the series, he was hitting over .300, but besides a monstrous home run and some clutch doubles, we knew we still hadn't seen it all from Chip, and I think his teammates sensed the same, and so, before that seventh game even started, me and the press boys were mapping out our scenarios.

"I say he goes 4 for 4 with 4 bombs over the right field fence!"

"I say...mark this one down, that he does the unexpected: Three triples, a single and a winning steal of home!"

"Nah...two homers, a game-saving play at first, and a kiss from Elly at home plate while he holds the trophy!"

"Listen here," I said, "now it's my turn, and I say he hits three homers, knocks in all the Tiger runs, but his last homer will be in the ninth inning, right when all the fans think that hope may have already gone into hibernation for the winter."

We were all wrong. Of course we were. You cannot guess what Doolin's going to do, because he always does more – he always *did* more, excuse me. None of our scenarios included the squirrel either. That's right, a baby squirrel. The one that ran onto the field when the Pirates had loaded the bases in the seventh inning and the momentum was theirs for the taking. The umpire, the groundskeepers and

THE ADVENTURES OF CHIP DOOLIN

even some fans tried to run the squirrel off the field, but to no avail. He kept running back to the second base bag where he'd sit atop it like a king, next to base runner, Tommy Leach. Jim Delahanty tried to coax it with nuts, and Sam Crawford even tried to throw his hat on it. But it was the farm boy, Doolin, who knew what to do, but we'll get to that in a minute, because a whole lot of other fireworks and excitement occurred before that, and all of it surrounded, guess who?

It started in the first inning. With old friends, Jimmy and Clyde sitting in the front row beside Eleanor, Doolin came to the plate with two outs, against starter Babe Adams, who was vying for his third win of the series. Chipper didn't waste any time. Not even a single pitch. The first one Babe Adams threw him, Chip launched over the right field fence, to give the Tigers a 1-0 lead. It was the start of a very economical day for the star first bagger.

In his next at-bat, that came in the third inning, with Donie Bush dancing off first, Chip hit the second pitch he saw that day over the centerfield wall for a two-run home run, scattering those geese I had mentioned. Two at-bats, two pitches...two home runs. The crowd went wild...until the top of the fourth inning. That was when the Pirate offense erupted like a volcano!

With the score 3-0 and Tiger starter Bill Donovan

on the mound, the Pirates quickly loaded the bases with nobody out. That was when Fred Clarke walked; then Honus Wagner drove in two with a single and Dots Miller followed with a two-run double. They scored twice more and before the top of the fourth frame was done, the Pirates had a commanding 7-3 lead!

When Chip walked to the plate in the bottom of the sixth inning, with Ty Cobb on second, the crowd gave him a standing ovation for the hitting display he had put on thus far, to their overwhelming delight, but now they were begging him to do it again, this time to restore their hope and enthusiasm. By now, one would have thought that Pirate starter Babe Adams would have known better than to challenge Chip again, especially with first base open, but his pride must have gotten the best of him. When Chip settled into the batter's box, Adams wound and delivered, and when he did, he let out a loud grunt that sounded like a horse; that's how determined he was to get Chipper out. However, on the first pitch of the at-bat, again, Chip hit a bomb that sailed over the left field fence for an opposite field two-run homer, his third of the game...on three successive pitches, bringing the Tigers to within striking distance, 7-5.

In the top of the seventh – yes, that's when the wondrous squirrel appeared, sent down there by Mother Nature or the Almighty himself – the Pirate momentum died before everyone's bemused eyes, and maybe their season too, thanks in part to that little critter, nature's talisman to the Tigers. As I mentioned earlier, the Pirates had loaded the bases with nobody out, on two singles and a walk, and the dangerous Honus Wagner was due up next. Everyone, even Hughie Jennings, expected the Pirates to tack on *at least* two more runs with Wagner coming to the plate. George Mullin was the Tigers pitcher, having come on in relief of Bill Donovan, and just as he climbed the hill to get ready to throw, seemingly out of nowhere, a baby squirrel scurried in from shallow centerfield, perhaps from under the Bennett Field grass, and sat right on top of the second base bag.

The home plate umpire, Silk O'Loughlin, yelled for time.

"Hey, Leach!" he said, yelling to base runner, Tommy Leach, "chase that squirrel off that bag or he'll interfere with the game and you might twist an ankle."

As soon as Leach went for the critter, it started running in circles around his feet, as if playing a game of chase! Leach bent over and tried to grab it, but it ran right through his legs. This went on for at least a few moments, until Leach actually appeared to tire from the ordeal! Fred Clarke, who was the runner at first base, came over to try and help out his teammate. He figured he and Leach could corner the baby fella, but to the entertainment of the crowd, the squirrel jumped past them and darted about, right when they made a swipe for it. Clarke ultimately lost his balance and fell to the ground.

After Delahanty tried using the peanuts and after Sam Crawford tried to throw his hat on it, both to no avail, Chipper entered the ordeal and made it look easy.

"Now I been watchin' you fellas try and corral this here poor squirrel. You been doin' it all wrong. All's you have to do is this…"

Chipper proceeded to get down on all fours. He lowered his head to the baby squirrel and we all watched his lips move, as he started talking softly to the animal. Now squirrels can be quite vicious and even dangerous, but this here was a baby, and a smart, spry one at that!

"Hey, lil buddy," said Chip, "how's you doin'? We got a World Series goin' on here, and right now, you're the center of the attention in this whole ballpark, and maybe in the whole doggone state of Michigan! Are you lost from your home? If you are I sure knows a bit about that…you see, I know your kind from spendin' long days on my papa's farm, and…"

Chip must have been on the ground talking to that squirrel for about twenty long minutes, all while the fans, the players, both managers, the umpires, the concession boys and all the press, looked on in quiet captivation. No one bothered him. No one interrupted. And slowly, the squirrel took a liking to Chip and nuzzled his nose to Chip's nose, and by the time Chip had finished, the squirrel was all curled up in a small, furry ball, in the palms of his hands. He got to his feet and calmly walked off the field, through the bleachers and the ticket gates, and out onto the street, where he placed the squirrel, ever so gently, in a nearby tree.

"Now I certainly wish you to have the best squirrel-life of any squirrel. I thought it best to put you here for safe keepin'. Now you be good and watch them carriages that go fast past here. Okay?"

Chip then tipped his cap to the squirrel and re-entered the ballpark.

When the game resumed, the Pirate threat was extinguished with a single pitch from George Mullin to Honus Wagner. Mullin fired a fastball on the inside half of the plate. Wagner turned on it and hit a line drive bullet right at the Tiger third basemen, Charley O'Leary, who on instincts alone, speared it – saving his life in the process – then threw to second, doubling up a flat-footed Leach; Bush then threw to first, where Fred Clarke was called out on a close play, thanks to a valiant stretch by Doolin, completing the triple play! Jennings leapt with joy in the dugout, as the Detroit fans erupted with cheer.

The Tigers were still trailing 7-5, when Chip walked to the plate in the 9th inning, with nobody out. Cobb was on first base after hitting a ringing single off Adams, which made Chip the potential tying run. When player/manager Fred Clarke saw Doolin walking to the plate, he made a pitching change, summoning Lefty Leifield to pitch against the lefty-hitting first bagger. While it was a good thought that Clarke had, it really didn't matter, because the first pitch Leifield threw to Chipper, he knocked it out of the park in right field, for a game-tying two-run homer, his fourth of the game!

After putting runners on first and second – and the game-winning run in scoring position – Leifield finally got out of the jam when he got Boss Schmidt to pop out. Game seven was suddenly going to extra innings. The heartache for the Pirates was that since the Tigers had two base runners after the home run, Chip Doolin's turn at the plate was coming around yet again; he was the fourth hitter scheduled to bat in the 10th inning.

The Pirates went in order in the top half of the 10th, and it took Mullin just 10 pitches to do it. The bottom half started off with a boom for the Tigers, as Tom Jones, pinch-hitting for Mullin, hit a double in the left-center field gap to get things going. Leifield then walked Donie Bush. The next batter, Ty Cobb, hit a little nubber off the end of the bat that squirted between the pitcher's mound and third base; Leifield didn't even try to throw the speedy Cobb out at first, and the bases were suddenly jammed for the hero of the ages, Chip Doolin.

The sky was still sparkling with sunshine. Fans were still gripping their programs, now even tighter with victory in their sights. They all rose to their feet for Doolin. The culmination of his first pro season was this at-bat. Everything was vibrant...from the rich color of the dirt around home plate, to the silky black fedoras on the heads of the fans, to the smells of baseball and immortality.

A curious thing happened when Chip dug into the batter's box amidst the flashing bulbs of cameras. The whole park went silent. It was the type of silence that is often reserved for music or show performers; musical maestros or someone teeing off in a game of golf. It was a show of respect for the man at the plate who had so far demonstrated a skill unmatched by anyone on earth. It was a wanton silence. The hearts of the fans and also of the writers who *wanted* to see one more...who wanted to see that apropos ending, the one that only the man at the plate could supply. There wasn't a single sound. Not even from the players. No one. Not from the base runners either. No cheering him on. Not from the pitcher or the catcher, for their hearts had already sunk.

Leifield tried to delay the inevitable. He threw, "Ball one!" Then, "Ball two!" They were the first two balls Chipper had taken all day. He stepped out of the box, looked to the skies and spoke softly to himself. He later told me what he said: *This one's for you, Pop.*

There was no stopping him that day. Not the greatest pitcher then...or now. He was immortal. Leifield tried to sneak a tailing fastball over the inside corner of the plate, knee high. It looked like a darn good pitch, one that would have gotten past any other hitter, but Chip. When I saw his hips open up, I knew it was gone. And I think Leifield knew too, even before the barrel of Chip's bat hit the ball.

Chip Doolin's fifth home run of the game, a grand slam, was hit so hard and so high, it sailed over the right field bleachers, out of the park and to somewhere unknown. The ball was never found. The rookie first bagger catapulted the Tigers to World Series champions, in a stunning 11-7 victory. For the day, his stats read like this: *5 for 5, 5 home runs (1 grand slam), 5 runs scored, 11 RBIs; part of a game-saving triple play in 7th inning.*

When Chip crossed home plate, he was hoisted up, onto the shoulders of his Tiger mates, and paraded back around the field, along the bleachers,

THE ADVENTURES OF CHIP DOOLIN

where he exchanged handshakes, hugs and well-wishes with the Tiger fans, who had also poured onto the field in celebration. When he came back around, down the third base line, he spotted a very beautiful sight: Eleanor was standing on home plate waiting for him. His Tiger mates brought him to her. The photographer bulbs flashed and lit up the ball park once again, when Chip gave her an extra special hug...with tears flowing.

"You hit that for your Daddy, didn't you?"

"Yes, darlin', I sure did."

"Well, Chip Doolin...you're the greatest ballplayer on planet earth. And your papa is probably sitting in the front row of Heaven with that ball on his lap, with a big, wide smile across his face."

When their lips met in a kiss, it became an instant front page photo on every newspaper and magazine cover, under a common headline, *The World Champion!* Like I say...he was the best ever.

The day after that first season ended, he signed his first endorsement deal, for milk. He appeared in an advertisement urging children to drink their milk:

> *Knowledge is important.*
> *Never stop learning.*
> *Never stop reading.*
> *And drink your milk...it's the stuff of*
> *Champions!*

NEAL D. BOGOSIAN

The heroics never ended, season after season, day after day...not until that fated day of which we all must face, and now you know the story of Chip Doolin. Tell it to others so they don't forget. Teach them what you now know...tell it from the beginning: *Let me tell you about a man named Doolin. Chip Doolin was his name and he was one of the finest gentlemen to ever play the game of baseball, and boy could he hit!*

CPSIA information can be obtained at www.ICGtesting.com
Printed in the USA
BVOW070314121011

273430BV00001B/192/P